Personal Word from the Author

Dearest Readers,

Thank you so much for choosing one of my books. I am proud to be a part of the team of writers at Tica House Publishing who work joyfully to bring you stories of hope, faith, courage, and love. Your kind words and loving readership are deeply appreciated.

I would like to personally invite you to sign up for updates and to become part of our **Exclusive Reader Club**—it's completely Free to join! We'd love to welcome you!

Much love,

Brenda Maxfield

BRENDA MAXFIELD

VISIT HERE to Join our Reader's Club and to Receive Tica House Updates!
https://amish.subscribemenow.com/

CONTENTS

Personal Word from the Author	1
Chapter 1	4
Chapter 2	15
Chapter 3	24
Chapter 4	33
Chapter 5	44
Chapter 6	49
Chapter 7	59
Chapter 8	70
Chapter 9	82
Chapter 10	91
Chapter 11	97
Chapter 12	108
Chapter 13	119
Chapter 14	126
Chapter 15	133
Epilogue	140
Continue Reading...	145
Thank you for Reading	148
More Amish Romance for You	149
About the Author	151

Chapter One

> Righteous lips are the delight of kings; and they love him that speaketh right.
>
> — PROVERBS 16:13 KJV

Daniel Studer looked furtively around before dashing into the library at Linder Creek. He simply couldn't let anyone see him, and his uneasiness made him jumpy. It was always this way. For four months, he'd been sneaking about like someone trying to escape the law. Which wasn't the case at all.

Not exactly, anyway.

He wasn't hiding from the *Englisch* law, for sure and for certain. But he was breaking the *Ordnung*. There was no avoiding that truth. When he'd first agreed to this, he hadn't truly considered all the ramifications. He'd only wanted to help his cousin Freddie out of a major problem. Not that he'd been totally in favor of it, even from the beginning. But Freddie had pleaded with him.

"You don't understand," Freddie had said, grabbing Daniel's arm. "I can't go to *Dat* and *Mamm*. *Dat* would wring my neck. He'd disown me. But I've got to have the money."

"How am I supposed to get that kind of money? I don't have it, Freddie. And the only way I could get it would be to ask my *dat*."

"*Nee*," Freddie had cried, alarmed. "He'd go straight to my *dat*. Can't you get it somehow. I'll give it back—"

"How and when? Huh? You can't get that kind of money, either."

"I'll get it somehow. I just can't get it fast enough for right now. C'mon. Help me out. I'm your kin."

"Don't try to make me feel guilty," Daniel had said. "I'd help you if I could, but I can't."

"*Jah*, you can." Freddie had stared at him hard. "You could write them articles."

Daniel stiffened. He never should have told Freddie about that. Never. He should have kept his mouth shut. "I'm not doing that. I already told you. It'd be considered a sin."

"*Nee*, it wouldn't. Plenty of Amish folks write articles for the newspaper."

"Not in Hollybrook, Indiana, they don't. And not for secular tabloids."

"You don't have to use the word tabloids. You make it sound worse than it is. You told me it was an online newspaper. So what? People read newspapers online all the time."

Daniel had leaned closer. "Not Amish people."

"I'll go to jail again."

Daniel sighed heavily. Freddie had asked for it, but Daniel's heart couldn't be so cruel. He knew his cousin well. Freddie talked tough, but he wasn't tough. Daniel had heard stories of what happened in jails. His cousin would never survive.

"You need to go to the bishop."

Freddie looked at him as if he'd lost his mind. "I can't do that!"

"You were drinking and driving, Freddie. Own up to it and things will somehow work out."

Freddie's eyes filled with tears. "You don't have to remind me what I did. But it could have been a lot worse. I could have hurt someone. I learned my lesson, Daniel. Truly, I did. I won't ever do it again. I have to pay Sean back the bail money. And I'll need money for legal stuff. And I need to pay for the car."

Daniel's heart twisted. He and Freddie were more like brothers than cousins and had always been there for each other. Since Daniel was the older of the two, he'd continually looked out for Freddie. It was only during the last year that things had changed. Freddie had turned twenty-one, and even though his *rumspringa* was long over and he'd promised to join church, he hadn't settled down.

Daniel suspected he'd only promised to join church to get his father off his back. For Freddie continued to hang around with the *Englisch* friends he'd made during *rumspringa*. When Daniel had warned him of the dangers, Freddie had ignored him. And now, here they were.

Freddie had been drinking and driving a friend's car when he'd run into a tree. The police had come, and Freddie was hauled to jail. Freddie had called Sean, the owner of the car. Sean had bailed him out, but that was only the beginning of the nightmare. Freddie's court case was coming up, and he was petrified of going back to jail. In truth, Daniel didn't know that much about the *Englisch* court system—the inner workings of it, so he had no idea of all that was involved. Why should he?

He'd never in his life known someone who'd been arrested.

But now, he did. His own cousin.

"Please, Daniel. If you write them articles, they're going to pay you big. You told me, remember?"

Indeed, Daniel had told him. He'd been approached by a man when he'd been leaving a hardware store in Linder Creek, around two hours by hired van from Hollybrook. The man, Scott Mason, had pulled him aside and asked about the Amish. At first, Daniel had been affronted and hadn't said much, but the man's sincere manner lessened his hesitancy.

The man asked Daniel to collaborate on a series of articles he was writing about religion. He told Daniel he would be commissioned to write the articles on the Amish with some guided questions, and Daniel would be "paid handsomely." Scott Mason would also need photos. Daniel had rejected the idea, even though he knew how to use a computer because of his family's woodshop business, as they were allowed to use computers for business purposes.

But certainly not to write articles. And not to provide prohibited photos that would invade their lives.

And certainly not to write about his own people in his own district. Daniel didn't have to inquire to know what the bishop's answer to that would be. When Scott Mason had mentioned the amount he would be paid, Daniel was certain he hadn't heard correctly, but he had. After turning Scott down and traveling back to Hollybrook, Daniel was still so stunned by the incident that he'd told Freddie.

And now it had come back to bite him.

"No one would have to know. You could just write the articles and get paid." Freddie eyes were still full of tears. "I won't ask again. I promise you."

Daniel had allowed Freddie to wear him down. And now, here he was, four months later, still writing. He didn't want to admit it, but he enjoyed it. From the first, he'd enjoyed the writing side of it all. But what was enjoyment when it was burdened with guilt?

And Daniel did feel guilty.

No one knew what he did when he went off to Linder Creek for the day. Daniel didn't dare use the computer in his family's woodshop in Hollybrook to write the articles. He couldn't risk being discovered. So, he used a computer in the Linder Creek library, far enough away that no one should ever see him.

But he'd told Scott this was his last article, for he simply couldn't do it anymore. Enjoyment or not, the guilt was eating him alive. And because of that guilt, he hadn't provided Scott with as many photographs as he wanted. How could he?

As promised, he'd turned over all his earnings to Freddie. He had no idea exactly how they were used. He did know that his cousin wasn't in jail. Daniel hadn't asked questions. In truth, he didn't want to know anything further about it. He was already too involved as it was.

He sank into his usual chair in the computer lab of the library. He always chose the computer furthest from the door, in the back of the lab, where the only way someone could see him was if they purposefully went over there.

He logged on with the free visitor's code given to him every time he came. His mind went to Anna. Dear, beautiful Anna. He paused and smiled. They had spent a wonderful evening together the night before. He'd taken her riding. The February evening had been unseasonably warm, well into the fifties. Sometimes, the weather did that in Indiana. Warmed way up or cooled way down, seemingly independent of the seasons. In any case, he and Anna had taken advantage of it and gone for a drive together. They'd even stopped at Edmund's Pond and taken a walk.

His heart warmed at the thought. He had asked Anna to marry him right there at the pond's edge. And she'd said yes. *Ach*, but it had been a wonderful night. Some folks had guessed they were courting, even though they'd done their best to keep it private. But soon, everyone would know. They'd have to wait a bit to be published, but privately, they could begin dreaming and making their plans.

Had Anna told her parents yet? Daniel wasn't sure. She had a close relationship with her mother, so it was likely she had.

Anna was going to be his. This loving, faithful woman whose shining brown eyes crinkled up when she giggled. This sweet woman who lived to help others and loved to make people happy. *His* Anna.

He stared at the computer and his stomach turned over. What was he doing? He shouldn't be here. This should have been long over. No. It should never have begun. He shouldn't be writing under the false name of Mark Tupper. Still, he owed this one last article since he'd already been paid for it. He brought up a blank document and poked at the keyboard until the title appeared: *One Man's Questions in the Face of Authority*. And then he typed, *Written by Mark Tupper.*

This last article was a completely new idea from Scott. Daniel knew without a doubt that the man was intentionally stirring up controversy. He was hoping Daniel would hit hard, causing people to question everything. It gave Daniel a bitter taste. The cursor blinked at him, taunting him to begin the article. Daniel glanced at his notes on the subject and realized he couldn't do it.

He couldn't keep this up any longer. It was wrong. If he was found out, it wouldn't go well. Could he be shunned? He could. Or at the very least, he would be disciplined.

Was he really helping Freddie by rescuing him? The question had plagued him more than once over the last few months. Was he making things worse in the long run, with Freddie not having to face what he'd done without Daniel's help? What was the right thing to do? Daniel had prayed about it, but he wondered if he'd really heard God's answer.

Because right then, the overwhelming sense that he was wrong threatened to drown him. He abruptly stood, nearly knocking over the chair behind him. He gaped down at the computer screen. He wasn't going to write this last article. He couldn't. He'd pay Scott Mason back the money he'd already been given for it. He didn't have that much money right then, but he could get it if he sold the grandfather clock he'd made as an engagement gift for Anna.

He cringed. These last couple months, he'd put his heart and soul into the building of that clock. He'd never made one before, and it had taken him months and months of cutting and sanding and gluing and...

But was any cost too high to be in integrity again? Right then, he thirsted for feeling right again. He craved it. He swallowed hard. He would sell the beautiful clock he'd just finished and free himself. He was glad Anna hadn't yet seen it; it wouldn't be right to take something away he'd already given.

He took a deep breath and bent down to log off the computer, but he wasn't quick enough.

"Daniel?"

Daniel froze. Turning slowly, he saw Deacon Elias walking toward him.

"D-deacon?"

"What are you doing here?"

Daniel blinked and nausea swept through him, settling like a rock in his throat. Deacon Elias was the strictest, harshest deacon in their Hollybrook District. What was *he* doing here?

As if he'd asked out loud, the deacon said, "Matthew Weiger and I came to post news of the horse auction. I thought I saw you standing in here. What..."

His eyes jumped to the computer screen that now glared like a blinding spotlight.

"What's this?" the deacon asked, pushing Daniel aside. "You working on this? Is this yours?"

Daniel was so overcome, he couldn't utter a sound.

"Who's this Mark Tupper?" The deacon's forehead scrunched over his brow as he leaned even closer to the computer screen.

Daniel held his breath, feeling ready to pass out.

The deacon straightened. "What are you doing?"

Lie, Daniel's guilt urged him. He opened his mouth, but he couldn't do it. Bad enough to have written the articles. But to lie on top of it? No.

"I'm writing—"

"What?" the deacon interrupted. "You're writing? What do you mean?"

"I've been writing articles on faith and the Amish way of life for a ... a newspaper—"

"What?" the deacon said, his scathing tone not much above a whisper.

"I-I'm sorry. I was just going to quit when you came..." Daniel's voice faded as he heard how ridiculous he sounded. The deacon would never believe that, even though it was true.

"What newspaper?" The deacon's eyes narrowed. "Not our area's Amish newspaper? If so, why wouldn't you use your own name?"

"*Nee,*" Daniel admitted. "A newspaper on the computer. It's... It's owned by *Englisch*. I-I've been writing for a paper that is only read on computers and cellphones.

The deacon flinched and gaped at Daniel. "You... Daniel, you..." He was momentarily without words, but he recovered soon enough. "I'll take this up with the bishop and the people." He shook his head, his anger now replaced with rebuke. "You'll have consequences."

"I know that," Daniel muttered, knowing he deserved to be disciplined. "I—"

"Spare me the details. I've heard enough. You'll put an end to it *now*," Deacon Elias said. He gave him one last censuring look and then turned on his heel and was gone.

Daniel collapsed into the chair, his mind reeling. How was it that the minute he decided to quit, he got caught? He swallowed the bitterness that rose in this throat. He'd known all along he shouldn't be writing these articles. Though he had allowed his cousin to talk him into it, it wasn't Freddie's fault. It was his own fault. Pure and simple. It was he who had done it. Freddie hadn't held a knife to his throat.

A trembling started deep within him. How had he—Daniel Studer—gotten into such a mess? Daniel had always been faithful to his district and to the *Ordnung*. Always. He considered himself a good, loyal member of the community. Never in a hundred years would he have believed he could go so astray.

What was Anna going to think? He let out his breath in a rush. Anna, dear, dear Anna. What would she think? They were engaged now. She was engaged to someone who had committed a grievous sin against his faith.

He turned to the computer and logged into his email. *Email.* He had an email account that had nothing to do with the family business. It was his and his alone to communicate with *Englischers. Ach,* but how far he had strayed. His stomach twisted as he dashed off a note to Scott Mason, telling him he couldn't do the last article. Indeed, he couldn't do any more articles ever. He closed his note by promising to repay the money he now owed.

He logged off and switched off the computer. He stood and blindly left the library. He made no attempt to check and see if the way was clear. To see if anyone might see him.

It was too late. It was much too late for that now.

Chapter Two

❦

Anna hummed as she helped her mother clean up the kitchen. Margaret Mast looked over at her daughter and smiled.

"You're right chipper this morning."

Anna grinned, unable to help herself. "*Ach, Mamm.* I'm so happy."

Margaret squeezed out the dishrag. "As well you should be. Daniel Studer is a fine young man."

"That he is," Anna agreed. She put up the last stack of clean plates and turned to her mother. "Were you this excited when you were first engaged to *Dat?*"

Margaret laughed, her face flushing slightly. "*Ach,* I was over the moon, daughter. I couldn't wait to marry my first love. We didn't have a long engagement. He asked me to marry him, and we were published within two weeks. The wedding was two weeks after that." She chuckled. "I thought my *mamm* would have a heart attack. We hardly had time to make the *newehockers'* dresses or my wedding gown."

"Some still have very short engagements," Anna said.

"That is true. But now, I believe, a lot of young folks are secretly engaged before it is ever published. I thank you, Anna."

"For what?"

"For not keeping this a secret from me. Now, we shall have a *gut* long time to make your wedding dress and to plan everything. And I'll be planting a lot of celery for the wedding supper."

Anna laughed. "Should I tell *Dat?*"

Her mother bit her lower lip.

"*Mamm!* You already told him!" Anna accused, though she wasn't upset about it.

"Of course, I did. And you'll do the same thing after you're wed. You'll tell Daniel everything, too."

"I s'pose you're right," Anna said. "Was he happy?"

"He was right pleased," Margaret said.

"*Gut.* He likes Daniel, *ain't so?*"

"Of course, he does. All the folks around here like him. He's a *gut* lad, and he will make you a *gut* husband."

Anna put her arms around herself, still grinning widely. "I can't wait, *Mamm.* Truly."

"Well, you'll have to wait. But you'll be surprised. The time will go by right quick."

"I hope so. We'll likely be living in his family's *daadi haus* at first," she said.

"I figured as much. It's a shame this old farmhouse don't have one. I'd have liked you to live here with us."

"It'll be easier over there, what with the woodshop there and all."

"So Daniel will keep working with his *dat*?"

"He will. He likes it." Anna put the bag of flour back under the counter. "He isn't much for farming. I know *Dat* thinks farming is *Gott's* real work..."

Margaret laughed. "You're right at that. But he's not so foolish as to know others are called to different work."

"I'm just so excited. You think *Mammi* will be happy?" Anna paused. "Or did you already tell her, too?"

Margaret shook her head. "*Ach*, daughter. I can keep a secret. Just not from your *dat*. Your sisters will be pleased."

"I hope so. Is it all right if we don't tell them right off?"

"That's your decision, Anna. Though Prudence and Maggie and Sandra will all be happy for you."

"I'm going to ask them to be my *newehockers*. But I want to wait a little while."

"You have time to wait a while. But we'll have to get started on the dresses before long. Then, they'll have to know."

Anna nodded. Her mother was right, but she wanted to hold her secret close for a bit longer. It was such a delicious, wonderful thing, and she wanted to revel in it quietly.

Just then, Prudence came into the kitchen. "*Mamm*, Maggie and Sandra and I have gone through all the seeds in the barn. We made a list, so you know what to order."

"Thank you," Margaret said. "We'll want a big garden this spring."

"We always have a big garden," Prudence declared. At sixteen, she'd already proven to have quite a green thumb. She looked at Anna. "You going to help plant this year?"

"I always do."

Prudence laughed. "*Jah*, I s'pose you do. Although, I don't think you like it much."

"Maybe not. But since when does liking something have any sway. The garden still needs planting, and it's too much for you and Maggie and Sandra alone."

Margaret raised a brow. "Let's not forget that the mother around here does her share, too."

They all laughed at that. Anna gazed at Prudence with affection. As Anna was ten years older than Prudence, she had played a big part in raising her. Indeed, she had with all three of her younger sisters. She warmed at the thought of someday having her own children to raise. Hers and Daniel's. Heat rose up her neck at the thought.

"What's the matter with you?" Prudence asked, studying her. "You sick?"

Anna blinked. "*Nee*. I'm perfectly fine. Let me see the list you made."

"Maggie's got it. She and Sandra are still in the barn."

"Are we finished here, *Mamm*? Can I go on out?" Anna asked.

"Go on with you. I'll tend the last bits."

Anna smiled and ran outside with her sister toward the barn. Anna was still so distracted by thoughts of Daniel and the wedding that she even forgot to put on her coat.

Daniel stood at the end of his family's drive after the Mennonite driver of the hired van dropped him off. Had Deacon Elias beaten him back to Hollybrook? Had he already been to Daniel's home, relaying the bad news? Daniel swallowed with difficulty. He was twenty-nine years old. Old enough to be considered for deacon himself. During the last opening in Hollybrook, enough people had voted for him for him to be put in the lottery.

Shame burned through him. What if he had chosen the correct hymnal that day—the one decreeing him as deacon. Would he have helped Freddie out then? Would he have broken the *Ordnung* then?

No. He wouldn't have. The knowledge increased his shame. Shouldn't he have the same behavior and attitudes of a deacon whether he was one or not?

Did his faith mean so little that he would compromise it? He sighed heavily.

At the time, he'd only thought of Freddie. Helping Freddie. The way he always did. But Freddie should have never asked him. Never. Did Freddie think so little of Daniel as to pull him into his mess?

But Freddie loved him, didn't he? They were like brothers.

As Daniel stood there, his confusion grew. He hadn't considered it quite like this before. If he had, he might have saved himself all this anguish. Because right then, he saw things in a completely new light: *Freddie had used him.*

Even as Daniel railed against the revelation, he knew it to be true. His cousin had taken advantage of their relationship. With Daniel's ill-gotten money, Freddie had paid whatever was necessary. He'd taken care of things so that his life could go on as before.

But Daniel's life would never go on as before. Not now. Anna's sweet face hovered in his mind. *I'm sorry, I'm sorry, I'm sorry*, he thought. He prayed his discipline would be short-lived. That it wouldn't interfere with their engagement. *Ach*, what was he thinking? Was he trying to get out of things just like Freddie? He blew out his breath in a huge sigh. Then he squared his shoulders and walked toward the house.

He needed to tell his parents before he was called to the bishop's. Or before the deacon came calling. It wouldn't be fair for his parents to be caught unaware. *Ach*, his mother would weep, for sure and for certain. He felt like weeping himself.

He opened the side door and walked into the washroom. He slipped out of his coat and his heavy shoes and went in through the kitchen. His mother was at the stove, stirring something. She looked over and smiled, and then the smile fell from her face.

"*Ach*, what is it? What's happened?" she asked, her face losing its color.

His mother was like that. She knew things before any words were spoken. She could sense when something was wrong before anyone else did.

"I need to talk to you and *Dat*," he said.

"Your father's out in the woodshop. Go fetch him." She turned off the burner and set the pot aside.

He turned and went to put his shoes back on. He hurried to the woodshop and asked his father to come inside.

"Why?" Aaron Studer questioned. "I'm in the middle of something here, and it—"

"Please, *Dat*," Daniel said.

Something in his tone must have conveyed the gravity of the matter, for his dad immediately set down his chisel and followed him back to the house. Back inside, Daniel asked his parents to sit at the kitchen table. He, himself, didn't sit; he was too nervous. As it was, he shifted his weight back and forth from one foot to the other.

"Tell us, son," his mother said, her face now completely drained of color. "It's bad, *ain't so?*"

"It's bad," Daniel said reluctantly. "I'm going to be disciplined."

There. It was out. His parents gaped at him, their mouths now open in shock.

"What?" Aaron asked. "What do you mean? What for?"

His mother had gripped the edges of the table. "What have you done?"

"I-I have been writing articles for a computer newspaper. Using the computers at Linder Creek Public Library. I've been doing it under a false name. Today, Deacon Elias walked into the library and caught me."

On her chair, his mother swayed and for a split second, Daniel feared she'd pass out, but she righted herself.

"Deacon Elias?" she murmured. "*Ach, nee*. Not him."

"What was *he* doing there?" asked his father.

"Putting up information about the auction..."

Ruth Studer swirled to face her husband. "What difference does it make why he was there? He was there! He caught our son in sin." She turned pleading eyes to Daniel. "Why? Why were you doing it?"

"I needed the money," he said, wondering if he still needed to keep his reasons secret. But hadn't he basically promised Freddie he would?

"Money?" cried his father. "What for? And why not ask me for money?"

"I-I couldn't," Daniel said, hating that he couldn't explain it all. But right then, in some twisted way, he felt that if he could at least keep his promise of silence, he wasn't completely without integrity.

"Why not? Why couldn't you? What have you done?" His father was standing now, and a flush was creeping up his face. "How much money?"

Ruth was shaking her head. "Wait. Wait. How in the world did you even know about this article writing? This don't make any sense at all."

"I was approached by a publisher," Daniel said. "I turned him down. Of course, I did. At first. But then something happened, and I had to get money quickly."

His father's face screwed up in angry confusion. "For what?"

"I-I can't say. To help someone."

"To *help someone?*" Ruth cried, her voice rising in pitch. "By breaking the *Ordnung*? By going against all you've been taught?"

Her tears had started now, and Daniel's stomach twisted with regret. This was so wrong. What he was doing to his parents. Never had he felt so low. So disgusting.

"I'm sorry. I made a mistake," he said. "I thought I was helping. I should have never agreed."

"I want to understand this," his father demanded. "This is going to reflect on all of us."

"Will our Daniel... Will he be shunned?" his mother asked, looking up at her husband.

Aaron blinked hard. "*Nee*. I don't think so. *Nee*."

"Then what will happen?" she asked.

"I don't know," he snapped and then sank down on the chair. "Daniel, you'd better start talking. You'd better tell us the whole story."

"I can't," Daniel said. "Not yet. I-I need to talk to someone first."

"Son—" his father started.

But Daniel was already leaving again. He needed to talk to Freddie. He needed to tell his cousin what had happened.

Chapter Three

Daniel rode his bicycle to his aunt's and uncle's house. He figured he still had another hour or so of daylight. That was enough time to tell Freddie and then go back home. He walked right into the house without knocking as was their custom.

"Why, Daniel, what a nice surprise," his aunt exclaimed as he entered the front room.

"Hello, *Aenti*. Is Freddie here?"

"He's up in his room. Shall I call him?"

"*Nee*. I'll go on up."

"Will you stay for supper?"

He paused. "*Nee*, I'll need to get right home."

His aunt looked disappointed, but she didn't argue. Daniel nodded and then went up the stairs two at a time. He pushed into Freddie's room. Freddie jumped up from the bed where he'd been lying.

"Daniel, what are you doing here?"

Daniel carefully shut the door behind him. "I got caught."

"You ... what?"

"Deacon Elias knows about my writing. He knows about my false name."

Freddie's eyebrows shot up to the top of his head. *"What?"*

"I'm to be disciplined now," Daniel said. "My folks want to know why I suddenly needed money, and—"

"You didn't tell them, did you?" Freddie cut in. "You didn't say anything, did you?"

"*Nee*," Daniel said. Looking at Freddie's earnest expression, he suddenly knew this wasn't going to go the way he'd hoped. Freddie wasn't going to confess about the accident and drinking. "But I need to tell them why I did it. I just wanted to warn you first."

"*Nee*," Freddie cried sharply. "You can't tell them. It's all over now. My folks know nothing. If you tell your folks... If you say anything, *Dat* and *Mamm* will find out."

Daniel strode one step closer to where Freddie stood. "Are you hearing me? I have to tell them what happened. The deacon might already be at my house."

Freddie shook his head. "*Nee. Nee.* You can't say anything. It won't help things. You're already in trouble. Why bring me into it?"

Daniel stared at his cousin's begging expression. He saw the way Freddie was blinking quickly. He saw the fear in his eyes. And something inside Daniel curled and shriveled. Freddie wasn't who Daniel had always thought him to be.

Had this been reversed, and had Daniel needed Freddie's help, Freddie wouldn't have come through for him. Deep sorrow shook him as he realized the truth of it. Freddie would have left Daniel to scramble through it on his own.

Just as he was doing now.

"I did this for you," Daniel said slowly. "All of this was for you."

Freddie licked his lips. "And I'm grateful. You saved me, cousin. But now... Now, I have nothing to do with this. It's out of my hands." He leaned forward. "Don't you see? I didn't write anything. You did that. And you can't talk about the arrest. You promised. You can't tell."

Daniel couldn't stop gaping at his cousin. Anger tugged at him, and he did his best to shove it aside.

Freddie was not going to help him out.

Daniel took a step back and then another. And then, saying nothing further, he left the room, but not before hearing Freddie cry, "Don't say anything! Daniel! Don't! You promised!"

Daniel hurried down the steps, barely gave his aunt a farewell wave, and raced from the house, jumping onto his bicycle. He pedaled hard and fast, his cousin's words ringing in his ears. Never again. Never, never, *never again* would he try and help Freddie out.

Yet Freddie admitting his part in things wouldn't completely help. Daniel knew that. Except Freddie's admission would at least explain it. Explain Daniel's reasons. Daniel still had to own up to his own actions, but then, if his folks could see his motivation—they would know he was trying to help his cousin.

He could still tell his parents. He could. He could tell them all about Freddie's accident—his night in jail.

But would he?

Dearest Lord, *what was he going to tell Anna?*

He pedaled harder until he'd worked up a sweat despite the cold air. He needed to see Anna right away. He had no idea what his discipline would be. Would he be silenced? If so, he wouldn't be able to talk to Anna.

Ach, but he'd made a right mess of things.

He slowed his bicycle and turned around, now heading for the Mast home. He knew Anna wouldn't like him coming straight to the door; he'd always met her at the end of her drive, keeping their meetings secret. But today, there was nothing for it. Besides, she'd probably already told her mother about their engagement.

He groaned as he pedaled. Had he destroyed that, too? Had he destroyed their engagement with his foolish decision?

He swung his bicycle into the Mast drive, nearly slipping on a patch of ice. He pedaled directly to the front porch, jumping off and letting his bicycle fall to the ground. He leapt up the steps and knocked on the door.

Margaret Mast opened it. "Why... Daniel." She seemed at a loss for words, and then she smiled at him—a lovely warm smile that stretched from ear to ear. "Come in, son. I'll fetch Anna."

He blinked. "Um, can you have her come out here to talk?" He didn't think he could bear another second of Margaret's warm welcome. Just wait until she heard about everything he'd done. And she would hear, too. Everyone would. The whole district would be involved in his discipline and the tongues would wag.

Margaret gave him a puzzled look. "All right, Daniel." Her smile faded. "I'll go get her."

Daniel backed away from the door. Margaret shut it and within minutes, Anna appeared, pulling on her coat.

"Daniel?" she said, her eyes filled with worry. "What is it?"

"I-I need to talk to you," he said. "I didn't want anyone to hear."

"But we're riding out tonight, *ain't so?* It couldn't have waited?"

"*Nee,*" he said. He looked at the porch swing. "Please sit down."

She gave him a wide-eyed look. "All right," she said softly and sat on the swing.

He licked his lips. "Um. Something has happened—"

"Are you breaking up with me?" she interrupted, her hands pressed to her chest.

"*Nee,*" he said quickly. "But you might want to break up with me."

"Never!"

He inhaled deeply. His stomach hurt. He felt sick. "I'm to be disciplined..."

She gaped at him. "What? Disciplined? What do you mean? What for?"

"Deacon Elias knows something... He's going to tell the bishop. I'm to be disciplined."

Her eyes were wide and questioning. "I-I don't understand."

He told her what had happened, only leaving out his reasons.

"Wait. But, but why? Why did you need the money? I don't understand why you would do such a thing." She kept shaking her head, her confused brown eyes latched onto his.

"I can't tell you…"

She sprang up from the bench. "We're engaged, Daniel! *Engaged*. Doesn't that mean that we can tell each other anything?" Her forehead scrunched with bewilderment. "Why would you be writing articles? You must have had a *gut* reason. You have to tell me…"

He inhaled sharply. She was right. They *were* engaged, and she deserved to know. More than anyone, he reasoned. More than anyone, she deserved to know.

He sank onto the bench beside her. "It-it was for Freddie."

"Freddie? Your cousin, Freddie? Why did he need money?"

As he told her, her eyes grew every wider with each word. "So… So, you did this for him?"

Daniel nodded. "I see it was a mistake now. I should never have agreed."

"Do Freddie's folks know?"

"No one knows."

"Then, he has to tell them."

"He won't."

"Then you will."

"I gave him my word."

Anna set the swing in motion, rocking back and forth, back and forth, almost frantically. "So what happens now?"

"I don't know. I go home and wait."

Tears filled her eyes, and her gaze pierced into him. He sucked in his breath. "I'm so sorry," he said, his voice breaking. "I'm so sorry."

She blinked back her tears. She looked down at her hands. "Are you, really? Are you sorry?"

Her tone wasn't normal. It was on edge, tight.

"Of course, I'm sorry."

She sniffed and raised her chin. "We'll wait then. We'll wait for the deacon and the bishop."

"I *am* sorry..."

She looked at him again and the swing abruptly stopped. She stood. "Thank you for telling me. Can you... Can you let me know what happens? Soon? Before preaching service?"

He nodded, feeling something shift between them. He shuddered, his heart full of lead. How could he have brought this shame onto all of those he loved? How?

She gave him a smile that faltered badly and then turned and walked back into the house and shut the door.

He hesitated for a long moment. And then with a sigh, he got up, went down the steps, and got back on his bicycle.

Anna shut the front door behind her and leaned heavily against it. Disciplined? Her fiancé was to be *disciplined?* His sins would be broadcast throughout the district. Every single person would know what he had done ... and no one would know why.

Resentment toward Freddie Wagler burned through her. He had no right to ask Daniel to do such a thing. How could he have done it? Had he no regard for Daniel?

And Daniel had agreed.

Daniel was too kind and loving and supportive. Yet, those were some of the very things she loved about him. But this? How could he have agreed?

Ach, but everything was a mess.

"Anna?" Her mother asked, coming toward her. "Is everything all right?"

Anna stood straight. She forced a pleasant expression to her face. "Everything's fine, *Mamm,*" she said, and then before she could burst into tears, she went flying up the stairs to her room, not even bothering to take her coat off first.

She threw herself on her bed and let the tears come freely now. She was such a jumble of emotions; she couldn't think straight. Anger, love, resentment, pity, and shame all twisted inside her. She'd never personally known anyone who'd been disciplined. Not well, anyway. But it did happen on occasion, and it was always a big deal, and it was always horrifying to whomever it directed toward.

And now it would be directed toward Daniel. Her dear, dear Daniel.

His family would be devastated.

Ach, Daniel, why did you do it?

And he hadn't just done it once. He'd continued writing for four months. Four *months*. Which meant that he'd been involved with it during all those weeks of courting and had never said a thing to her. Nor had she ever suspected all was not well.

If he could deceive her like that…

She shivered. It didn't bear thinking about… But she couldn't *stop* thinking about it. It spiraled through her mind like a pervasive root. Did this mean he would deceive her after they were married, too? And why wouldn't he? *Ach,* Daniel.

He wasn't who she thought he was. She rolled over on her bed, and she couldn't stop the sobs from coming. Were her dreams gone now? Was it all over?

What would happen?

She put her arms around herself. She loved Daniel. She needed to support him. To be loyal to him. But he had deceived her.

She squeezed her eyes closed. Daniel. Daniel. Daniel.

Chapter Four

Daniel set the bicycle against the barn wall and walked to the house. He saw his mother at the window, watching him. The look on her face was enough to break his heart all over again. He went around to the side door and was just opening it when he heard a buggy approach and pull to a stop. Everything in him froze as he slowly turned and saw Deacon Elias and the bishop get out of the buggy.

He took a deep breath and went to meet them.

"Bishop," he said.

The bishop's face was tight. Deacon Elias grunted his greeting and the three of them silently walked up the front steps. Daniel opened the door and ushered them into the house. His father and mother were standing inside, and they looked like statues.

His father visibly swallowed. "Deacon. Bishop," he greeted them, his voice stiff.

"Aaron," the bishop replied. He gave a slight nod to Daniel's mother and then walked straight into the front room to sit down on the davenport. The deacon followed and sat on the other end of the davenport.

Aaron and Ruth scurried after them, sitting in two rockers. Daniel braced himself and joined them. The only place left to sit was between the bishop and the deacon, and he didn't dare do that, so he remained standing.

"I-I can get you tea," his mother stammered.

The bishop looked at her. "This ain't a social call."

"Our son has told us what he's done," his dad said. "We know there will be consequences."

The deacon gave Daniel a scathing look which he felt down to his toes. The bishop's look was not as hard, and Daniel saw the sorrow in his eyes.

"So, it's true then?" the bishop asked. "I've heard what Deacon Elias had to say, and it's not that I doubt him. But I wanted to hear from you, too, Daniel."

Daniel's throat was so dry, he could barely swallow. "It's … true. I've been writing under a false name on the computer."

"The deacon never told me why, except he said you needed money. I'm confused on this, Daniel. Your folks could have lent you money. If it was an emergency, we have the district fund. What was it that you needed this money for so badly that you would compromise yourself?"

Daniel rubbed his hand over his mouth. "I-I can't say."

The effect on the bishop was the same as if Daniel had yelled the words. He flinched, recoiled, and then stared at Daniel.

The sorrow Daniel had seen earlier disappeared, and in its place was censure. Deep and full and thick.

"You ... what?" the bishop said.

"Daniel," his father cried. He looked at the bishop. "I'm sorry, bishop. He wouldn't tell us either." His father turned entreating eyes to Daniel. "Tell him, son. Tell him. We need to understand this."

Bile rose in Daniel's throat. He was going to choke. Uncertainty raged through him. What was he to do? He couldn't deny the bishop, could he?

But what was his word worth?

"I-I gave my word," he said.

The bishop stood. "Daniel Studer, I expect you to tell me your reasons."

"Daniel," his mother murmured, her eyes full of tears, "tell the bishop."

Daniel tried again to swallow. His throat didn't seem to be working properly.

The bishop took a step closer to Daniel. "I expect you to tell me your reasons. Don't make this worse than it already is. If you disregard me wholly, I will have no choice but to take the vote to the people for shun—"

"*Nee!*" his mother cried. She jumped up and rushed to Daniel. "Tell him. You *must* tell him."

Daniel's eyes burned with tears. "I..."

His father stood. "You must answer to the bishop. Will you shame us like this? You've been taught our ways. You know what to do."

And Daniel did know what to do. The bishop was the final authority in the district. Would Daniel now make his sin worse?

He squeezed his eyes shut. Despite what he had done, he was Amish to his very core. He couldn't do it—he couldn't ignore the bishop's demand.

"I did it for Freddie," he blurted.

"Freddie?" both his parents cried.

"What do you mean, Freddie?" his father asked. "Freddie Wagler?"

"Why did he need money so badly?" his mother asked.

The bishop sat back down. His father and mother did the same.

"Tell us what happened," the bishop said. His voice was calm.

Daniel told them, watching his parents' eyes grow wider and wider. When he was finished with the story, he was surprised to feel a sliver of lightness in his spirit. Even with the situation as it was, he felt better for the telling.

His mother dabbed at her tears with the corner of her apron. "I understand," she murmured. She turned to her husband. "It makes sense now. They've always been so close."

But Aaron Studer's face was hard. Daniel winced. Didn't his father believe him? Or was he simply angry with him?

Deacon Elias cleared his throat. "It still ain't no excuse for what you've done."

"I know that," Daniel said. Oh, how he knew it.

"I see you're repentant," the bishop said. "This will go a long way in determining our course of action. There will likely be a public confession after preaching service."

Daniel squared his shoulders. He had expected no less. "*Jah*, Bishop."

The bishop stood again, as did everyone else. The bishop and the deacon took their leave, and Daniel was left standing there, facing his parents.

"Your cousin will be disciplined, too," his mother said. "I can't imagine the bishop will let that go by."

Aaron turned and left, returning quickly with his coat. "I'm going to see Bart and Minnie. They need to know."

Daniel cringed. So Freddie's parents were going to know, after all.

This just got worse and worse.

Anna was certain the whole district would know what Daniel had done, and it likely wouldn't take that long. It was shocking how quickly news could travel, even without the advantage of modern technology. And if the whole district knew, then her parents would soon know, also. She would rather they heard it from her.

The morning after Daniel told her, she went downstairs to find her parents. She also gathered her sisters. They might as well hear it from her, too.

"I... I have to tell you something."

Anna looked at her mother's worried face. How Anna wished she was announcing something about her engagement, instead of her beau's moral failure.

"Are you gettin' married?" eight-year-old Sandra blurted. "Maggie is sure that's it."

"Why else would we be having a family meeting right now?" Maggie said, a wide smile on her face.

"Can we be your *newehockers*?" Prudence asked. "Sisters are usually *newehockers*. *Mamm*, can we all get new dresses?"

Margaret frowned. "I don't think that's the announcement, daughters. Give Anna a chance to speak."

Anna licked her lips and took a breath. "Daniel... Well, you all know Daniel is my beau. We tried to keep it a secret, but..." She took another breath. "Daniel will be coming up for discipline, likely this Sunday at preaching service."

Margaret gasped softly and pressed her hand to her mouth. Her father stood. "What? What are you talking about?"

Tears burned the back of Anna's eyelids, but she willed herself not to cry. She forced herself to explain all that had gone on; the decision Daniel had made; what he'd done.

Her father had gone stiff. He was staring at her. "And... And you're engaged to him." He wasn't asking, for he already knew, as her mother had told him.

"I knew it!" Maggie cried and then clamped her mouth shut.

John Mast inhaled sharply, once, twice. "You will go visit your *aenti's* home in Linder Creek."

"Wh-what?" Anna stammered. "But why?"

"Are you questioning me, daughter? You will do as I say."

THE BROKEN ENGAGEMENT

"But *Dat*—"

"John?" Margaret interrupted. "Why are you sending her away. She's done nothing."

"*Nee*, she hasn't. And she ain't going to be engaged to someone who blatantly ignores the *Ordnung*." He walked to the large wooden bureau at the side of the front room. He opened a drawer and took out the envelope where Anna knew he kept cash. He pulled out some bills.

"I'll be buying a bus ticket, and I'll give you some cash for emergencies. You'll stay with my sister until this has blown over." He strode back across the room, stopping in front of Anna. "You'll call off the engagement."

"John!" Margaret cried.

Anna's mouth dropped open, but no sound escaped. She'd known her parents weren't going to be happy. She'd known that. But for her father to demand that she break up with Daniel? No. No. *No*. She couldn't do that.

"Do you hear me, daughter?" John asked, his voice firm. "I will not have you tied to that man. I know you think I'm being harsh. But this is for your own *gut*. You'll be leaving right away."

Anna could barely nod. Her stomach twisted, and she felt sick. She glanced at her sisters. They were gaping at her, their eyes wide.

Her father cleared his throat. "Go on upstairs and pack. The bus leaves at ten o'clock. Or at least it used to. If it don't, I'll hire a van to take you."

Anna turned pleading eyes to her mother. Margaret looked as stunned as Anna felt. Anna sucked in her breath and then ran from the room, taking the steps two at a time up to her room.

She shut the door behind her and sank onto her bed. She had to *leave Hollybrook?* She had to live with her aunt? She'd never been fond of Claire Mast. Claire was a harsh, opinionated old woman, who was quick to cast judgment on anything she didn't favor.

And she would *never* favor Daniel. Not after this.

Was Anna's engagement really over? Just like that? With a few words from her father? *Ach,* would even she be allowed to at least see Daniel before she left? Daniel wouldn't know where she was or what had happened. Anna reached over to the drawer on her nightstand, pulling it open and taking out her tablet and a pen. The least she could do was write him.

She squeezed her eyes shut and tears dripped down her cheeks. *Daniel.* Her beloved Daniel. How had this happened? She opened her eyes, and her hand shook as she began to write.

Dear Daniel,

When you get this, I will be gone. Dat *is insisting I go stay with* Aenti *Claire in Linder Creek. He says our engagement is over.*

Anna gulped back her sob.

I must leave today. I can't bear the thought of not seeing you before I go, but I dare not try. Dat *will not look kindly on it, and I don't want to upset him any further.*

As you can guess, I told my family what happened. About you writing on the computer. I supposed they were going to hear about it anyway, and I wanted to be the one to tell them. I thought it would go better if they heard it from me. I told Mamm *about our engagement and she told* Dat. *So when I shared the news, they were both upset.*

Daniel, Dat *is angry. I hope,* nee, *I pray that with time he'll calm down and allow me to come home and allow us to continue with our engagement plans. Do you know what your discipline is to be yet?*

I will pray for you. I will pray every day this will all be over soon.

Daniel, please write to me. I'll put my aenti's *address at the bottom of this letter. I will try to get to the mail each day before her to see if you've written. Otherwise, I fear she will not give me your letters. Don't put your return address on the envelope. That way, maybe she will give them to me not knowing they're from you. She's a hard woman, my* aenti. *And I know* Dat *will tell her what has happened, and she'll be in complete agreement with him that the engagement is over.*

Gut-bye, dear Daniel. Write to me.

All my love,

Anna

Anna stumbled a bit over her closing. She did love Daniel, but right then, she was heartsick over what he'd done, and she didn't feel completely loving. And that bothered her deeply. If she couldn't be completely loyal, completely true, with all her mind and heart when things were bad, didn't that mean something? Didn't that mean her love was somehow faulty? That she had failed Daniel in some way?

She shuddered and again tried to wrap her mind around what was happening. She was meant to be filled with excitement that day. She was meant to be busy planning her wedding, or at least planning her bridal dress.

Instead, she was being shipped off to her aunt's house, away from her family, away from her friends, away from Daniel.

It wasn't supposed to be this way. She blinked back her tears, annoyed with herself now. Self-pity wouldn't change a thing. Not a single thing. It would only allow her to be resentful. And she didn't want that.

She quickly re-read her letter, jotted her aunt's address at the bottom and then folded it and stuck it into an envelope. She addressed it and then realized she'd have to go into the front room to find a stamp in the bureau. Could she do that without her father seeing?

A soft knock at the door startled her. She quickly stashed her letter under her pillow.

"Come in," she said, wiping her eyes.

Prudence pushed through the door and came over to the bed. "I'm sorry, Anna. Truly."

Anna's eyes filled with tears all over again. "Thank you, Prudence."

"I think... I've always thought... Well, I think Daniel is still a *gut* man." Prudence's eyes were so filled with compassion, Anna's throat tightened.

"H-he is..." Anna managed to get out.

"This will pass," Prudence said. "You'll come home soon. Won't you? *Dat* won't make you stay forever, will he?"

Anna struggled to put a smile on her face. "Of course not. I'll be home soon. This whole matter will become a memory." How she wished it would be so.

"I'll write to you."

"Thank you." Anna took her hand and squeezed it. "Prudence? Will you kindly get a stamp for me?"

Prudence gave Anna a look that clearly indicated she knew why Anna needed a stamp. She nodded and left the room. Within minutes, she was back and handed Anna the stamp.

"No one saw me," she said. She gave Anna a sad smile and left the room.

Anna pressed the stamp on her letter to Daniel and tucked it under the waistband of her apron. She'd get it into the mail somehow. But right then, she needed to pack. She pulled an old leather suitcase out from under the bed. It was battered and sagged as she laid it open on the bed. This suitcase had been used by everyone in the family for longer than Anna had been alive. Never, in her wildest dreams, did Anna ever think she'd be using it in such circumstances.

She tried to shove all thoughts out of her head except what she needed to pack, which in truth, wasn't all that much. A few changes of clothing was all. That and her tablet, some envelopes, and her pen. She'd have to figure out a way to get stamps in Linder Creek. Surely, her aunt wouldn't hold her captive in the house.

She shook her head and gave a soft snort. She wasn't going to prison, was she? She was only going to stay with her aunt.

But it felt like prison, nevertheless.

Chapter Five

Daniel couldn't sit still. He couldn't even stand still or stay in the house after the bishop and deacon left, and after his father stormed out to head to Freddie's. *Ach,* but Freddie was going to be angry at Daniel. Well, that couldn't be helped.

Daniel simply couldn't have made things worse by ignoring a direct demand from the bishop.

"I'm going out to the barn, *Mamm,*" he said, walking into the kitchen where his mother was standing at the counter, staring at nothing. She jerked at his approach and turned her sad eyes on him.

"All right," she murmured.

He went to her and put his hand on her shoulder. "I'm sorry, *Mamm.* I thought I was helping Freddie. I didn't want to, but then I did it anyway. I wish I could take it back."

She looked up at him, her eyes misted over. "I know, son. It will be all right."

He squeezed her shoulder and went through to the washroom to put on his coat and head outside. In truth, there was nothing much to do in the barn. He straightened the tools on the workbench and checked on the horses and the cow. He should probably head out to the woodshop instead, but for some reason, he hesitated. He didn't want to be out there when his dad returned.

Aaron Studer was sure to go out there himself, for that was where his father went in the evenings if anything was bothering him. Both Daniel and his mother always knew when he was upset, for after supper he'd head back out to the woodshop even though he'd already been out there all day.

The woodshop was his father's domain. Of course, Daniel worked out there with him most days, especially when the crops weren't planted. But still, it was his father's territory and Daniel wasn't about to invade it on a day like today.

Daniel had been out in the barn for nearly an hour when his father drove the buggy up the drive and came to a halt outside the barn.

"Daniel!" he roared.

Daniel's eyes stretched wide. What was this? His father never yelled out like that. He strode quickly to the barn door.

"What is it, *Dat*?"

"Come inside," his father said abruptly and headed toward the house.

He didn't bother to unhitch the buggy, which was odd in itself. What had happened now? He followed swiftly after his father, and they went into the house to the front room.

"Ruth!" his father hollered.

Ruth came scurrying out of the kitchen and joined them in the front room, her eyes wide and a look of dread on her face.

"Sit," his father ordered, and Daniel and his mother sat on the davenport. "I want the truth, and I want it *now*."

Daniel had no idea what his father was talking about, but by the look on his face, it couldn't be good. Daniel couldn't remember a time when he'd seen his father this agitated, this upset.

"I've seen Freddie," his dad started. "Bishop and Deacon Elias had just gotten there."

Daniel sucked in his breath. *Ach,* that meant Freddie was going to be disciplined, too. He thought of Freddie's parents... Daniel wished he could have saved them this pain, but there was nothing for it now. It was too late.

"They confronted Freddie, which I was about to do. Freddie says you're lying." He glared at Daniel.

Daniel jumped up. "What?"

"Freddie says you're lying."

"He... He... *What?*" Daniel couldn't possibly be hearing correctly.

"He said he had no idea what we were talking about."

"But... But that can't be—" Daniel cried.

"I want the truth *now*."

"I'm telling the truth." Daniel met his father's angry glare. "Everything I told you was the truth."

Beside him, still on the couch, his mother was weeping. He could hear her soft sobs, but he didn't break eye contact with his father. He had no earthly idea why Freddie would tell such a lie. And then a horrible thought gripped him. Had Freddie lied to him, too? His throat went dry, and he suddenly felt dizzy. Was this all a lie? Everything Freddie had told him?

And then he did waver. He sank to the davenport, his mouth open, shaking his head.

"Did he lie to me, too?" he asked, looking up at his father.

"It's easily checked," his father said. "Bishop and Deacon Elias are going to the police first thing in the morning."

"They're what?" cried his mother. "*Ach,* how can this be happening?"

Daniel turned to her and grasped her arm. "I'm not lying, *Mamm*. I'm not."

She looked at him, her eyes filled with tears. "I believe you."

His breath whooshed out of him. His mother believed him. But what was going on?

"*Dat?*" he asked, looking up at his father.

His father's angry stance slumped, and he suddenly looked old and tired. "What is Freddie up to? That boy has been rebellious for years, but what has he done?"

His father went to a rocker and dropped into it.

"Do you believe me?" Daniel asked.

His father took a long, slow breath. "I believe you. But the bishop and the deacon have doubts. They'll know soon enough."

"If it isn't true, then Freddie lied to me, too," Daniel said. "But I... I can't believe he would do that."

"He just lied to the bishop and the deacon, so why wouldn't he lie to you?" Aaron looked over at his wife. "That boy is no *gut*."

"D-don't say that," she stammered. "He's our kin."

"He's no *gut*, I tell you."

Daniel stood. "I'm going to go over there."

"Wait," his father said. "We'll go together. I want to hear this."

"He won't talk in front of you, *Dat*. I know him well. Maybe if I get him alone, he'll tell me what's really gone on."

"I don't like it."

"It can wait until tomorrow," his mother interrupted. "Maybe Freddie needs time to think things through. He and Daniel have always been close."

His father's eyes widened. "Have you been listening? Close? Nobody who's close would do such a thing."

"Give him the night," his mother insisted. "Please."

For a moment, it looked as if his father was going to spit, but of course, he didn't. Still, the disgust on his face seared into Daniel.

Ach, Freddie, what have you done?

"First thing in the morning, then." Daniel forced himself to say, not wanting to upset his mother further, but still wishing he could go that very minute.

Chapter Six

The next morning, Anna's father took her to the bus stop, which was really the parking lot of a local motel. When the bus came squealing to a hissing stop, she and her dad climbed out of the buggy. She reached back for her bag.

"Here," her father said, handing her a letter. "This is for your *aenti*. Give it to her when you arrive. I left a phone message for her in the shanty, but I have no idea whether she will have heard it by the time you get there."

Anna took the letter.

"Now, let's get you a ticket."

Since there wasn't a formal bus stop in Hollybrook, tickets were purchased directly from the driver. Anna stood there, hoping there wasn't a ticket left, which was ridiculous as she was the only one standing there waiting to get on—and three people had gotten off. Within minutes, her father returned and held out the paper ticket.

"Here you are, daughter."

"How long…" Anna swallowed. "How long must I stay?"

"Until you hear otherwise," John said. He sighed. "I'm not punishing you, daughter. This is for your *gut*. You won't have to be in the preaching service when Daniel is disciplined. Most folks know you're courting, or if they don't know it, they've guessed it. I won't have you subjected to the gossiping tongues. And there's going to be talk."

Anna didn't doubt that for a minute. She knew the ways of her people. Everyone knew gossip was a sin, but that didn't stop them from indulging in it. Yet, she wasn't a child. She was twenty-six years old, plenty old enough to maintain herself in the midst or wagging tongues. Her father seemed to have forgotten her age, for she felt like a child now, being shuttled off to her aunt's house.

"You'll write?" he asked.

Anna nodded. She'd already promised her mother. She would write them all.

Including Daniel, but her father didn't need to know that.

"I should get on the bus," she said. "*Gut*-bye, *Dat*."

It was an abrupt farewell, but she feared she might say something she'd regret if he continued to wait with her. Besides, the driver was finishing up his business of pulling three suitcases from the belly of the bus and putting hers in.

"All right, daughter. *Gut*-bye." John turned around and got back in the buggy. With a nod of his head, he snapped the reins and left the parking lot.

Anna waited another few seconds, and then she went running. Behind the bus near the motel, she'd spotted a blue mailbox. She could get Daniel's letter mailed right then, and he'd get it the next day. Much better than waiting until she got to Linder Creek to mail it. She hadn't dared put it in her family's mailbox where it could be discovered.

She pulled open the slot and dropped the letter inside. Then she ran back around the bus, slowed to a dignified walk, and got on. She found her seat easily as they were labeled with clear numbers on small metal plates. She was relieved when no one sat beside her.

A couple minutes later, the driver climbed back on and got the trip underway. Anna leaned her head against the back of the seat and watched Hollybrook disappear through her window. When all she saw were large expanses of frozen fields, she gazed down at her aunt's letter in her hand. She noted that her father had tucked the flap of the envelope in instead of licking it closed. Her thumb played with the edge of it and temptation rose like a wave inside of her.

She could open it and read it, and no one would know.

She sucked in her breath. *She* would know. God would know. Reading someone else's letter was wrong.

But was it a sin?

She bit her lip. Did it matter? Yet, it was wrong, and she shouldn't even be entertaining the idea. But she did entertain it. Would it be so bad to know what her father was telling his sister? It was about her. Didn't she have a right to know?

A right to know? *Ach,* but she was sounding like an *Englischer.* She stared at the envelope, and without allowing herself to ponder it a moment longer, she untucked the flap of the envelope and pulled the letter out, opening it.

. . .

BRENDA MAXFIELD

Dear Claire,

I left a message on your closest shanty phone, but I'm writing this, too, in case you don't get the message. I trust you will welcome Anna into your home for a while. I don't rightly know how long.

We've had some trouble here. Anna's beau had a moral failure—writing articles on a computer for an Englisch *newspaper. He's to be called before the church come Sunday. I didn't want Anna to be here for that. Many in the district know she and Daniel are courting. In truth, they were engaged, but I put a stop to that.*

I'm sure you'll agree that getting her out of Hollybrook is in her best interest. She needs to forget about this man. He is clearly no gut.

Put Anna to work however you think suits. I'll be in touch.

John

Anna let out her breath slowly. So. There it was. Her father had no respect for Daniel anymore. She pressed a hand to her chest. What was she to do? By the sound of his letter, her father would never change his mind. But he *had* to. Anna was going to marry Daniel. He was her true love.

Tears burned the back of her eyelids, and she blinked them rapidly away. She needed to get ahold of herself. As she'd thought before—she wasn't a child. She'd face this head on and somehow get her father to change his heart toward Daniel.

As she stared out the window, she didn't see the passing scenery anymore. The image filling her mind was Daniel's face, his tender eyes, his warm smile. Her heart stirred at the image, but as the miles wore on, something else crept in. Something besides love and admiration and compassion.

She didn't want to acknowledge it. She didn't want to admit it was there again. But it was.

Resentment. Resentment toward Daniel for making such a foolhardy decision. Had he given no thought whatsoever as to how it could affect her? Affect them? Had he no idea how this would play out?

She closed her eyes and took a deep breath. Resentment would help nothing. Not even a little bit. With sheer determination, she shoved it aside and tried to think of nothing at all.

Daniel grabbed his coat and hurried from the house the next morning. His father had already hitched the buggy, so Daniel got in immediately and snapped the reins. He was underway within seconds.

He yanked up on the reins in front of his aunt's and uncle's porch. Were the bishop and the deacon truly going to the police that day? Surely, that would clear Daniel's name of lying. The police would have a record of everything—the accident, the night in jail, the court proceedings.

What was Freddie thinking? How could he hope to get away with his lies? It would be all recorded at the police station.

Daniel jolted out of the buggy and leapt up the steps. He didn't bother to knock as it wasn't their custom. He burst into the front room and saw Bart and Minnie. They were hunched in their rockers, their heads close, talking. They broke apart immediately as he strode in.

"Where's Freddie?" he asked. Then he paused and took a breath and started again. "Hello, *Aenti* and *Onkel*. Is Freddie here?"

Bart stood. "Why are you here? Haven't you caused enough trouble?"

Daniel bit back the quick retort that sprang to his lips. "I'm here to straighten things out," he said carefully. "Is Freddie in his room?"

Minnie's hands were scrunching a fold of her apron. She nodded, but Bart said, "Whatever you say to him, you can say in front of us."

Daniel took in a long slow breath, working to compose himself. "I'm sorry, *Onkel*, but I need to see him alone."

Minnie reached up and tugged on her husband's shirt. "Let him go, Bart."

Bart glared at Daniel but didn't protest further. Daniel turned and left the room, taking the stairs quickly. He pushed through Freddie's door. Freddie was standing there, waiting for him.

"I figured you'd come," he said.

"What are you doing?" Daniel asked. "Why did you lie?"

"Why did you say I'd been arrested?" Freddie countered.

"Because you *had* been arrested?"

Freddie shook his head. "*Nee.* I wasn't."

Daniel blinked. "What? What do you mean?"

"I mean I wasn't arrested."

Daniel looked behind him to see if his aunt and uncle were there, but they weren't. "No one is listening. Why are you denying it? Do you know what kind of position you've put me in?"

"I'm denying it because it ain't true."

Anger surged through Daniel. "Freddie! Stop lying. You already told me the truth." He wanted to shake Freddie until his teeth came loose. What was Freddie *doing?* This was too much.

"It's not true. I don't know where you got such a story."

Daniel gaped at his cousin. "*Such a story?* You told me. I made that money for you. I was helping *you*."

"I wasn't arrested."

"Then why did you tell me you were?"

"I don't know where you got that story." Freddie raised his chin slightly, and Daniel clenched his fists to keep from hitting him.

He was breathing hard now. Confusion tore through him. Had he gotten it wrong? But how could he have? Freddie had *told him*. Daniel squared his shoulders.

"I'm not leaving this room until you tell me what's going on."

Freddie looked down at his feet. For a fleeting second, Daniel thought he saw guilt there, but then Freddie met his gaze again, and there was nothing there.

"Nothing is going on," Freddie declared. "You got it wrong. I think you were trying to give an excuse to make your sin not so bad. You know, soften up the bishop and deacon a little."

Daniel just kept staring. He couldn't believe what he was hearing. Was he in the middle of a nightmare?

"I'm sorry you're in trouble, cousin. If I can do anything to help, let me know." And with that, Freddie took a step back as if dismissing Daniel.

But Daniel couldn't move. His feet were stuck to the floor. His mouth was open, and he struggled to make sense of what was happening. He glanced behind him again, sure that his aunt and uncle were there, listening. They *had* to be there. They had to be the reason for Freddie's lies. But there was no one behind him. No one in the hall. No one listening in.

"You can help me by telling the truth," Daniel said, his voice now insistent.

"I *am* telling the truth. I, uh, I have things I need to be doing now." And with that Freddie turned his back to Daniel.

Daniel stood for a moment, fighting the urge to grab Freddie and whirl him back around. But despite his feelings, Daniel wasn't a violent man—he never had been, so he turned and walked out of the room. He nearly stumbled on his way down the stairs. He couldn't, for the life of him, imagine what had just taken place.

He left the house without a word to his aunt and uncle and hurried to get into the buggy. He picked up the reins, gulped in a breath, blinked back tears of frustration, and got the buggy underway. He kept sucking in breaths, trying to stop the dizziness, the confusion.

Don't worry, he told himself. *Don't worry. The bishop and deacon will get to the bottom of this at the police station. They'll know I'm not lying.*

THE BROKEN ENGAGEMENT

But something inside Daniel trembled. Something inside told him it wasn't going to be that simple.

∼

Daniel's gut feeling was right. By then, it was late morning. The cool winter sun shed reflections on the frozen ground when Daniel and his folks heard a buggy coming up the drive.

"*Ach, nee,*" cried Ruth. "What is it now?"

Daniel jumped up, praying it was Freddie come to apologize and fess up to his part in the whole mess. But it wasn't Freddie.

It was Bishop and Deacon Elias. They were ushered wordlessly into the front room.

Daniel looked at them with hope. But when he studied their expressions, his spirit plunged to his feet. This couldn't be good.

"We checked out your story," Bishop said, his voice stern. "Freddie was never arrested."

"*What?*" Daniel cried.

Deacon Elias gave him a scathing look. "Why make this worse?" his voice cut through the air. "Your list of sins is growing."

"I-I..." Daniel was flabbergasted. How in the world had Freddie managed to erase his police record?

Unless... Unless it wasn't true. He hadn't been arrested, and his reason for pleading for help and money had been a lie.

Daniel sank back into the davenport. Freddie had completely deceived him.

So, *why had he needed the money?*

Daniel's mother and father were both staring at him. Daniel shifted with discomfort. "I... I didn't lie," he muttered, knowing his words would do no good at all.

Deacon Elias spoke. "You'll be at preaching service," he said. "You'll need to confess and repent."

The bishop sighed. "It will go better if you do."

After the two men left, Ruth approached him. "Please confess, Daniel. Please. Otherwise, this will go on..."

Daniel looked at her, his heart breaking. "I will confess to what I did. But I won't confess to a lie I didn't tell."

He ignored her beseeching outstretched arms and headed up to his room. His stomach hurt. His head hurt. His heart hurt.

Freddie, what have you done to me?

He pushed through his door and shut it behind him. He sank down on his bed. "Anna, oh Anna. I wish you were here."

Anna's sweet soft presence was exactly what he needed. He ached for her words of love and kindness. He swallowed hard. What if she deserted him, too? It hadn't gone well when he'd told her what he'd done. What if she was finished with him? What if she broke off their engagement?

He put his head in his hands. He couldn't imagine his future without her. He loved her. He needed her.

Ach, please Gott, don't take Anna from me.

Chapter Seven

Anna got off the bus and glanced around. Her aunt was nowhere in sight, which meant she didn't know Anna was coming. Which meant she hadn't gotten the phone message. It wasn't a long walk to her aunt's place, but it was cold, and Anna would have to be careful not to slip on any ice patches at the side of the road.

Not that she was in a hurry to get to Claire's home.

As she set out, her mind went to Daniel. No resentment this time, just missing him. She wondered what he was doing right then. Dealing with all sorts of fall out, for sure and for certain.

Gott, please watch over Daniel. He is repentant, Lord. Let this all work out for your glory. And please, let my father's heart soften.

She had tucked her father's letter into her suitcase. She wished she could bury it in the frozen dirt by the side of the road, but she wouldn't dare do that. She took a deep breath of the icy air and trudged on. There weren't many homes along this road, just the occasional farmhouse perched in front of its sprawling fallow fields. Only a few cars passed her, and she was careful to step as far to the side as she dared without slipping into the ditch.

She was perhaps halfway there when she heard a buggy behind her. She slowed, but she didn't turn around. In truth, she wasn't in much of a mood to meet anyone. But her mood didn't matter, for she heard the buggy slow.

"Hello, there," came a cheerful male voice. "Can I give you a ride? It's awful cold this day."

She turned then and saw a young man, clean shaven—so, he wasn't married. He was alone in his buggy. He was smiling at her, a warm smile, making his blue eyes crinkle at the corners.

"I can walk but thank you."

She was ready to turn back when he said, "Where are you heading? It likely won't be no trouble for me to take you."

She inhaled, not wanting to reply, but that would be downright rude.

"I'm heading to Claire Mast's place."

He chuckled. "Then you're in luck. I live just beyond her. Come on. Get in. It won't take long from here."

She wavered but finally gave up and walked toward the buggy. He waited while she got in and reached behind to put her suitcase in the back.

"Looks like you're here to stay a spell. Are you kin?"

She nodded. "Claire is my *aenti*."

"I reckon she'll be happy to see you. She had a spill recently and hurt her ankle. That why you're here?"

This was news to Anna. "I-I hadn't heard."

He snapped the reins. "She'll be right glad to have you. My name is Luke Miller."

"I'm Anna Mast. Nice to meet you."

He grinned. "Same to you."

They went on in silence, the cold air in the open buggy still nipping at her. Right then, she longed for her closed family buggy with its propane heater.

"Where are you from?" He interrupted her thoughts.

"Hollybrook."

"Ahhh. I've been there before. My family was passing through a year or so ago. We'd hired a van to visit kin up in northern Indiana. We stopped in Hollybrook and ate at some café. I can't recall the name of it."

"We have a few cafés in town."

Luke had a pleasant voice and a manner about him which put Anna at ease. Her shoulders relaxed and she breathed easier as the buggy went down the road. She hadn't realized just how tense she was.

"If you need anything, you just holler," he said, and then he laughed. "Not literally. I don't think I'd hear you. But you can come by. Claire will show you where I live. *Nee.* I can point it out for you when we get to your *aenti's.*" He nudged her arm, which startled her. Goodness, but he was a friendly sort. "I live with my *mamm*, so no worries about coming to see a bachelor."

She blinked at him, unused to this kind of familiarity, particularly from someone she just met.

She nodded vaguely, not knowing how to respond.

"*Ach*, I'm a bit forward, *ain't so?*" He shook his head good-naturedly. "My *mamm* is always warning me about that. Can't help it though. I just like people."

She gazed at him. He said the oddest things.

"Don't know a stranger. Not me." He laughed again. "So, how long are you staying?"

How long, indeed. She wished she knew.

"I'm not sure."

"Well, no matter how long, you'll like it here. Folks are kind and *gut*. Our bishop is a fine speaker, too, so church shouldn't put you to sleep."

She gawked at him now. What kind of talk was this?

He chuckled. "The sermons can get long, *ain't so?* Haven't you ever been tempted to just close your eyes? Maybe for only a minute or two?

She just kept gawking.

"And then someone will cough, or your friend will give you a little shove, and you'll wake right back up? Usually with a big jerk. *Ach*, but that can be embarrassing."

He looked at her. "I've shocked you, *ain't so?* Weren't my intention. You seem like a nice sort."

She seemed like a *nice sort?* Her eyes widened, and then she couldn't help it. She burst out laughing. He laughed right along with her.

"There now. That's better. I figured you had a *gut* laugh in there somewhere."

She was shaking her head now. Goodness, but this man would keep a person on their toes.

"We're almost there." He snapped the reins again. "Now, I know your *aenti* quite well. And I'm sure I'm not telling you anything new, but she can be a bit on the gruff side. But her heart's pure gold. But anyway, I'm saying that if you need some cheering up, you know where to find me."

She let out her breath. "Thank you," she said, not knowing what else to say. She was tensing up again, though, as her aunt's place came into sight.

He touched her shoulder and then pointed beyond her aunt's small-ish white farmhouse. "Over yonder... See? The house over there. And the barn. That's my place. Mine and my *mamm's*. You come over anytime. My *mamm* would be right pleased to make your acquaintance."

He had been right. He wasn't far away at all.

"Thank you. I might just do that."

He turned into her aunt's drive. "I think I'll come in for a minute and give your *aenti* my regards." He gave her a sideways glance, his eyes dancing with mischief. "Unless, of course, you want to be greeting her in private."

Anna didn't want to be greeting her at all, but she said, "That'd be nice. And thank you for the ride."

"It was my pleasure." He gave her a wink and pulled up on the reins. "All right then. Let's go see how Claire is faring."

Anna got out, trying to ignore her trembling. Luke had already jumped out and circled around to grab her suitcase before she could. They walked up the porch steps together.

"With her ankle, I don't want her getting up to answer the door. Besides, I reckon as kin you would just go right on in." And with that, he opened the door and walked inside. She followed, somewhat slowly.

"Claire?" he called out. "It's Luke. And I've brought your niece."

"Luke?" came her aunt's familiar voice. "That you? My niece? What are you talking about?"

Luke went through to the front room, Anna still following.

"Anna, of course," Luke said, giving Anna a private surprised look as if questioning her aunt's memory.

Claire shifted herself on the davenport to sit up straighter. Her gray hair was slicked back tightly under her kapp, not one hair straying. Her weathered face was both curious and demanding. "Anna?" she said. Her thin, bony hands pushed down the quilt that she'd thrown over herself. "What are you doing here?"

"She's here to help you," Luke said easily. He glanced at Anna. "I'll put your suitcase down here, unless you want me to take it upstairs."

"Her ... suitcase?" Claire asked, her dark eyes settling on Anna with intensity.

"Wait a minute," Anna said, taking her suitcase from Luke. She opened it and dug out her father's letter. She took a deep breath and crossed the room, handing the letter to her aunt.

"What's this?" Claire asked, reaching out for the envelope.

"It's a letter from *Dat*."

"Ahh, so a surprise visit," Luke said, giving Anna another questioning look. "Um, I think I'll be going then. Anna, come on by sometime."

Anna barely heard him, for she seemed to be frozen under her aunt's stare. She did hear the front door open and shut, however, as he left.

"What's going on, child?" Claire asked, ripping open the envelope, despite the fact that the flap wasn't sealed.

"It's there in the letter. Um, how are you, *Aenti*?" she asked, sinking into the rocker opposite the davenport. She shuddered. It was cold in there. Wasn't the warming stove burning? She glanced at the little glass door and saw nothing but a few embers glowing. She got up and went to it, kneeling, and opening the door. She put in another log and poked it around a bit, stirring up the flames.

Claire had finished reading the letter. Her hand with the letter dropped to her lap. "I see."

Anna swallowed and went back to sit in the rocker.

"Why'd he do it?" Claire asked and there was no mistaking the disgust in her voice.

"He..." Anna bit her lip. She couldn't tell the whole story, for hadn't Daniel wanted her to keep silent about it? "He was helping his kin."

There. That didn't reveal too much, did it?

"His kin put him up to it?" Claire frowned. "What kind of family does this boy come from?"

Anna stiffened. "He comes from a *gut* family. Kind and faithful."

"Faithful?" Claire's brow rose to her hairline. "Don't sound too faithful to me. Your *dat* did right to end it and send you here."

Anna pressed her lips together. Couldn't her aunt be even one tiny bit compassionate? Was there no heart behind her stoic exterior?

"How's your ankle?" Anna asked, not wanting to discuss her beau another minute.

Claire glanced down to where it rested on the couch. "It's better. A right nuisance, it's been."

"I can help," Anna said. "*Dat* will be glad to know I've come at a *gut* time for you."

Anything to get the focus off the real reason she was there.

"I s'pose," Claire said slowly. "*Jah*. You're right. I could use the help. Not much, mind you. I ain't no cripple."

Of course, she wasn't.

Anna put on a smile. "*Nee, Aenti*, you aren't a cripple, for sure and for certain. Would you like some tea? I can bring you some."

Claire sighed. She made a rustling movement as if she were about to get up.

"*Nee, Aenti*. You stay put. I can find everything. And after I make the tea, I can fix us a meal. Would that suit?"

Claire looked about to protest, but then she sank back in the cushions. "Fine. Make yourself useful, child."

Anna fled the room. *Child?* Goodness, she hadn't been a child for years. Her aunt had a way of irritating her so quickly it made Anna's head spin. How in the world was she going to make it here, actually living with the woman? And without the rest of her family to cushion her aunt's impact. Anna was going to be the sole focus of Claire's attention.

She entered the spacious kitchen where the linoleum floors shone like glass. There wasn't a thing out of place. Not a crumb anywhere. She glanced around. There wasn't even a sign of food anywhere. It looked like a photograph from an *Englisch* magazine. Amazing how Claire kept things this tidy with a hurt ankle. The woman's strength of will was formidable.

Anna put on the kettle and found the tea and sugar. She knew Claire liked it unsweetened, but Anna felt the need for something sweet. She was going to have to fortify herself to survive here. She squared her shoulders as she went about her work. She could do this. And surely, she wouldn't have to be here long. Things would be straightened out in Hollybrook, and she'd be free to return.

And then she and Daniel could take up where they had left off.

Maybe Freddie had already stepped up and admitted his part in it all. That wouldn't erase what Daniel had done, but it might result in a softer punishment. Yes, surely Freddie had come forward and confessed his part.

Anna opened the refrigerator and poked around a bit, seeing what she could prepare for dinner. In truth, there didn't look like much. It was all tidy and in neatly stacked containers, but there wasn't much. And now that there would be two eating...

Anna needed to go to the store. She figured that was something Claire hadn't done since hurting her ankle. Did Claire still have Black? If so, the mare had to be well on in years.

The kettle whistled, and Anna prepared the tea. She carried the cups back to the front room.

"Here you are, *Aenti*," Anna said.

Claire reached out and took the cup. "You didn't put no sugar in this, did you?"

"*Nee*, I remember you like it black."

"*Gut*." Claire took a sip. "*Ach*, it's too hot."

"I'm sorry." Anna took a sip of her own tea, and it was too hot. She blew on it and took another sip. "I'm happy to go to the store for you if you'd like."

"Huh? The store?"

"I thought maybe you hadn't been for a while since you hurt your ankle."

"What? Why? Didn't find enough food to your liking in there? Did you open all the cupboards?"

Anna blinked, feeling attacked. "*Nee*. I-I just want to be helpful."

Claire snorted and took another sip. "I s'pose you're right at that. I haven't been to the store for a while. A few folks brought me a meal or two in the beginning, but not lately." She gave another snort. "Don't take long to forget an old woman like me."

"You aren't so old," Anna said. Truth was, Claire was probably no more than her mid-fifties, but her face told a different story. Perhaps her sour outlook on life had wrinkled her before her time. Anna had no idea. But she could see that folks would consider her old.

"Black needs a good brush down," Claire said. "I haven't been giving her the attention she's used to. You do know how to hitch up the pony cart?"

"I know how to hitch a cart," Anna said, affronted. What Amish girl didn't know how to hitch up a pony cart? She was disappointed, though, for the open pony cart in place of her aunt's closed buggy would make a cold trip to the store.

"You can make us a sandwich and then head into town."

"That sounds fine."

"I'll make up a list. You can put it on my tab. Get me my tablet, would you?" Claire asked, pointing to a tablet and pen lying on a side bureau.

Anna fetched them for her and then went back to the kitchen to prepare sandwiches.

Chapter Eight

Luke Miller unhitched his buggy, picked up the sack of flour he'd gotten for his mother and headed to the house. Before going in the side door, he glanced over his shoulder toward Claire Mast's place. So, her niece was here for a while.

Luke couldn't help but smile at the thought of Anna Mast. She was a pretty one. Awful solemn, though. Until he finally got her laughing. And then the melody of her laugh had washed over him, filling him with joy. He wanted to be the cause of her laughter again. There was something about her that pierced him straight through to his heart. He couldn't pinpoint it exactly, but there was a vulnerability about her, a sadness. He had no idea if something had happened, but it must have. For her visit to her aunt was clearly a surprise, and he was quite certain it had nothing to do with Claire's injury.

Which meant, there was something else. Whatever it was, it troubled Anna. He felt a compelling urge to ease whatever burden it was. Silly, he knew. Hadn't he just met the girl? Why in the world should he be driven to comfort her? To make her laugh?

It made no sense.

He chuckled. If he wanted to make her laugh, then so be it. He wondered what kind of excuse he could come up with to go visit her. He wished he could go right back over there immediately. See how she was settling in. See if she needed something.

He put his hand on the side doorknob. Goodness, but he had it bad. In just those few minutes together, he'd become smitten. About time, his mother would say. She'd been on him for months to start courting. But Luke hadn't found anyone who'd struck his fancy.

Until now.

Anna Mast. *Anna.* Even her name was melodious. *Anna.*

He went inside and delivered the flour to his mother who was punching down bread dough in the kitchen.

"You're back then," she said. "You took longer than expected."

"I gave a ride to Claire Mast's niece. She's here visiting."

"Ah, that's nice. She can be of help to Claire. I've been feeling badly that I haven't been over there for a few days."

"Would you like to go over later? I'll take you. and you can meet her niece."

Lois Miller paused. "Hmm. Might be nice, at that. I could take over a fresh loaf of bread. It'll be a bit, though. This is the second rising, and then it'll have to bake."

"Whenever you're ready, you let me know," Luke said, leaving the room with a satisfied grin on his face.

Anna had hitched the pony cart and was on her way. Her aunt's list of supplies and groceries was tucked under the waistband of her apron beneath her coat. She'd been right. It was cold in the open cart. No use complaining, though. Winter wasn't nearly over—not in Indiana. It could freeze well into May.

She shuddered. May. Surely, she wouldn't still be here in Linder Creek by then. Surely, by May she'd be back in Hollybrook, engaged once again to Daniel. She wondered what he'd think when he got her letter. As far as he knew, she was still there in Hollybrook. He wasn't going to be pleased; she was fairly certain of that.

Her mind flicked to Luke Miller. He was a nice sort. In a way, she felt like she already had a friend in him, which was surprising. They'd only just met, and he was a man. Whoever heard of having men friends? Especially as a single woman. But despite all that was going on in her life, he'd made her feel better. *Ach,* but the things he said. And the way he phrased things. She'd never known anyone like him. He was probably always fun to be around. For a flickering moment, she half wished she was still in his buggy with him. If anyone could make her forget her worries, it was him. She found herself smiling at the thought.

And then she came to her senses. Goodness, but what was she doing? Allowing herself to get lost in thoughts of another man? When her own dear Daniel was facing who-knew-what? She wasn't acting like much of a fiancée.

"You're *not* a fiancée," she muttered. "You're not even his girlfriend, according to *Dat.*"

Ach, that Daniel. What had he been thinking when he'd agreed to such an outlandish thing?

Once in town, Anna easily found the mercantile her aunt had mentioned. She parked the cart in the expansive lot and secured the reins. She jumped down and went inside. The wooden floor creaked as she began walking through the aisles. She'd never seen such a crowded store. The goods were stacked so high, she was certain they teetered—ready to topple at any moment.

"Can I help you there, miss?" asked a pudgy man with rosy cheeks. He wore a somewhat soiled white apron over his ample stomach.

"Um... *Nee,* thank you," she answered, returning his smile.

"You let me know, then..."

"I will," she said, watching him wander back toward the front of the store.

She'd taken a metal shopping cart to put her things in, and one of the front wheels simply wouldn't cooperate. She was about ready to give up when a young Amish woman approached her, laughing softly.

"You got *the* cart," she said.

"*The* cart?" Anna replied.

The woman laughed again. "*Jah,* the one with the wheel that has a mind of its own. Don't worry, we've all done battle with that rotten thing."

"I'm glad to know it's not just me," Anna said, laughing now, too.

"I'm Rose Stutzman."

"I'm Anna Mast, Claire Mast's niece."

"*Ach*, how is Claire doing? I thought to stop by this week."

"She's mending," Anna said.

"So nice that you're here to help her. I look forward to seeing you at the preaching service."

"Me, too. And it was nice to meet you, Rose." Anna appreciated the woman's friendliness. Maybe she would make lots of friends here, after all. It would certainly offset her aunt's sourness.

Anna continued doing battle with the stubborn cart until she went up to the counter to pay. She added the things to her aunt's tab as instructed and went back outside. She loaded the bags in the back of the cart and climbed in. With a flick of the reins, she was underway back to Claire's.

As she approached her aunt's place, her nose felt frozen. Her eyes had gone dry in the cold air, and she blinked rapidly. She hesitated at the end of her aunt's drive and gazed over the field of stubby harvested corn stalks to Luke Miller's place. She could barely make out some action near the barn. Was that Luke? She smiled. He was likely singing to his cow or something. He was just the type to be doing something like that.

She turned into Claire's drive and drove up to the barn. She jumped out of the cart and with cold stiff fingers—despite her gloves—she proceeded to unhitch Black. Oddly enough, a few moments into the task, she noticed she was singing.

"About time you got back," Claire called from the front room.

Anna hurried to her. "I got everything you asked for, *Aenti*. Would you like something before I start working on supper?"

"*Nee*, I ain't about to ruin my appetite with a snack." Her eyes narrowed and she surveyed Anna up and down. "Looks like you could do to gain a few pounds. You're downright scrawny."

"*Nee*, I'm not," Anna protested before she could stop herself. Goodness, but why in the world would she want to argue about that? "Maybe you're right," she added hastily.

That seemed to diffuse her aunt's criticism. "Of course, I'm right. Will you be frying them pork chops you just bought for supper tonight?"

"I'd be glad to," Anna said. "So, do you need anything?"

Claire shook her head. "You added the groceries to my tab?"

"I did. And I met Rose Stutzman while I was there."

"Did you now? She's a *gut* woman, is Rose. She ain't much older than you, but she's wed to a fine man." Claire emphasized the word *fine*. "A loyal and upstanding Amish man."

Anna knew where this was going, and she simply couldn't bear discussing Daniel with her aunt again. She was saved by a knock on the door.

"Who's that?" Claire asked. "I didn't hear no buggy."

"I didn't either." Anna hurried to the door and opened it to Luke Miller and a woman who had to be his mother.

"*Ach*, Luke. Hello."

He grinned at her. "Hello, Anna." He seemed inordinately pleased to see her. "I want you to meet my *mamm*, Lois."

Lois looked at Anna with the same shining blue eyes as her son. Her smile was warm and open, and she exuded friendliness.

"So, you're Claire's niece. My Luke has been telling me about you." She held up what appeared to be a loaf of bread wrapped in a dishtowel. "I've brought this to Claire. How is the dear?"

The dear? Anna nearly giggled at that. *Dear* would never be the way she described her aunt.

"Would you like to come in?" Anna said hastily, suddenly realizing that her guests were standing out in the cold.

She ushered Lois and Luke into the house and then directed them to the front room. Claire had jostled into a more upright position, having removed the pillow her foot had been resting on.

"Claire, dear, how are you?" Lois asked.

"I'm right *gut*," Claire declared, smiling. "Can't complain."

Anna thought Claire looked almost friendly when she smiled.

"Anna?" Claire continued. "Why don't you put on some tea." She looked at the loaf in Lois's hands. "What's this?"

"Some fresh baked bread for you," Lois said. "I'll take it into the kitchen for you."

"*Nee, Mamm*, I'll take it," Luke offered quickly, taking the loaf from his mother.

Anna had already turned to go into the kitchen to make tea, so Luke walked with her.

"So, are you settling in?" he asked.

"I've only just gotten here," Anna said, smiling. Her mood had lifted, and she wondered again at the influence this man seemed to have on her.

"*Mamm* was eager to meet you," he said, following her through the kitchen door.

"Was she?"

"She was." Luke placed the loaf of bread on the counter.

"Here, I'll unwrap it and you can take your dishtowel back."

"Whew," he said, with an exaggerated motion of wiping his forehead. "I was downright worried about that dishtowel making its way back home."

She cast him a quick glance and saw the mischief in his eyes. "I can understand your worry," she replied. "I dare say it's likely the only dishtowel your *mamm* has."

His eyes widened and delight covered his face. He laughed. "You're a teaser," he said with clear satisfaction.

Anna shook her head. She wasn't a teaser. She'd never been silly or humorous. She did have a sense of humor, of course. Didn't everyone? But she'd never been one to banter like this. Luke was getting the wrong impression of her...

Or was he simply bringing out something in her that had been there all along? Confused now, she turned toward the stove to turn on the burner under the kettle.

"If you need someone to show you around Linder Creek, I'm volunteering," he said. "You should know where the mercantile is and—"

"I've already been," Anna said, taking four cups and saucers from the cupboard.

"You've been to the store? Already?"

"Oh, I don't waste time," she said, with a lilting voice. Then she clamped her mouth shut. She was doing it again.

Luke leaned closer. "I never pegged you for a time-waster, Anna Mast."

Flirting. That was what they were doing. *Flirting.*

Shame ripped through her and again, she turned her back on Luke. With shaking hands, she got down the sugar bowl and a box of tea.

"Can I help?" Luke asked. "Not that I'm much help in the kitchen."

"But you do know how to eat." *Ach,* but where were these comments coming from?

Luke burst into laughter. "I'm a professional at that. You ought to see me. You'd likely want to applaud."

Anna swallowed. "I'm engaged to be married," she blurted.

Luke's brow rose and a bewildered look covered his face. "What?"

"I-I'm engaged. Or I was... I—" Anna stopped talking. What was she doing? She sounded ridiculous, stammering about like that.

"You're engaged?"

"*Nee. Jah.* Well, it's complicated."

He hadn't moved; he was staring at her. "So, you are? Or you aren't?"

Anna's mind rang with her father's words. *And she ain't going to be engaged to someone who blatantly ignores the Ordnung.*

"I guess... I guess, I'm not."

They stood regarding each other, and Anna felt completely lost. Was she not engaged? She'd just said she wasn't. But how could it really be over? Wasn't she writing to Daniel as if she were still his girlfriend? In her heart of hearts, didn't she still consider herself engaged?

And if so, why was she acting like this?

She shuddered. Life was confusing sometimes. And what was it about this man standing in front of her, studying her, that caused her to lose her bearings?

Luke's gaze softened, and he said, "That's *gut* to know, Anna."

"But..." She swallowed again, her throat scratchy dry. "I was engaged. My *dat* put a stop to it."

She was telling too much, but she found that she wanted to. She wanted him to know what was going on.

"Why?"

"He... Daniel—my beau—he did something wrong. Against the *Ordnung*."

Luke's brow rose. "I s'pose he had a *gut* reason for it," he said slowly. "I can't imagine you with a rebellious sort."

Her breath rushed out and she took a step forward. "*Jah*. That's it. He did have a *gut* reason. In his mind, anyway. He was helping his kin."

Luke tilted his head, still closely observing her. "But now he's paying for it."

"He's coming up before the church this Sunday."

Luke nodded. "That can't be easy."

Her eyes filled with sudden tears. "*Nee.* And I'm not there. I can do nothing to help."

"Anna," he said, his voice soft, "I reckon you wouldn't be able to do anything, anyway."

She sucked in a breath. "I know. But I should be there."

"So that's why you're here? Your *dat* sent you away?"

She nodded. "*Jah.*"

He let out a soft whistle. "I see."

"And I'm no longer engaged."

"Will he be shunned?" Luke asked. "Is it as bad as all that?"

"I-I don't know."

Luke shook his head. "I'm sorry."

She blinked back her tears and regarded him. "You've done nothing."

"I'm sorry you have to suffer through this."

Suffer through this... His words twisted in her. And again, she wondered why Daniel hadn't considered her when he'd made his decision.

Luke reached out and placed his hand on her arm—but only for the barest of seconds. "Shall we get the tea?"

"Anna!" came Claire's strident voice. "What's taking so long in there?"

Anna and Luke gave each other a meaningful look, and both of them laughed.

"You'll be on your toes, here," Luke said, smiling.

"That I will," Anna answered.

Together, they got the tea ready and then Anna sliced the fresh bread and buttered it, placing it on a plate. It was comforting working in the kitchen with Luke. Anna felt understood. Luke seemed to get it, and she was glad she'd told him.

When everything was ready, the two of them went back to the front room to serve the tea and bread.

Chapter Nine

Daniel gripped Anna's letter in his hand so tightly, the paper scrunched so that he could barely read the last of her words. Gone. She was *gone*. Her father had sent her away. Their engagement was *off*? A moan escaped him, and he sank to the edge of his bed. He read the letter again.

What a complete and utter mess he'd made of things. He'd put everything in jeopardy and for what? Now, Freddie wasn't admitting anything. And why had Freddie lied to him in the first place? Why had he needed the money?

The next day was preaching service. Daniel would be discussed after the service. He'd be asked to confess—and he would confess to what he'd done. But he wasn't going to confess and repent of a lie he hadn't told.

Would Freddie even be there?

And now Anna's father was completely against him. Anna would never marry him without her father's consent. He knew her well enough for that. Was it truly over? Had he really destroyed his own future? His and Anna's?

And his poor parents. What they must be going through. It was beyond thinking about.

He jumped up and began pacing his room. What could he do? What? The only thing he could think of was to force Freddie to tell the truth. But how could he do that? Freddie was determined to lie, and Daniel was only too aware of Freddie's stubborn nature.

Daniel strode to the window and looked out on the frozen yard. The towering oak tree stood naked and brittle-looking, stripped bare of its leaves. *Ach,* that was how he was going to feel the next day in church. And Deacon Elias would only be too eager to punish him. Would he be shunned? Surely not. He was going to freely admit his error and ask forgiveness.

But the lying?

Should he just admit to it, so that it could be over, and life could go on? No. No. No. It wasn't right. He couldn't admit to something he hadn't done. He had to preserve some of his integrity.

Dear God, what a mess.

The morning was starkly cold. Daniel had taken greater care than normal with his attire. He wore his cleanest shirt, his best suspenders. He even polished his shoes. It was ridiculous he knew, for it wouldn't make a bit of difference with how things would go. But it gave him something to do that morning, and he was determined to stand straight and tall. Not in a prideful way, to be sure. But with confidence.

Yet in truth, his confidence was flagging badly.

Breakfast was a dismal affair. His parents did eat, while he barely managed to get a bite or two down. No one said a word. No one looked at each other. The atmosphere lay over them like a stack of heavy quilts, pressing the air from the room. More than once, Daniel thought he was going to be sick, but he managed to force it back down.

After eating, he offered to help his father hitch up the buggy, but he was turned down. After the rebuff, Daniel stood in the middle of the room like the helpless, lost boy that he was. Later, upon arriving at the elder Yoders' barn for preaching service, he kept his gaze down. He only looked up enough to note that Freddie was indeed there, but when Daniel tried to catch his eye, it was useless. Freddie was going to let Daniel sink alone.

The feeling of betrayal nearly choked him. How could his cousin be so ruthless? And after what Daniel had done for him? Daniel could hardly stomach it.

The service that day seemed to go on for ages. The second sermon, always the longest, broke all records that day. The bishop was wound up, talking with such fervor that Daniel was sure he must be spitting onto the people in the front benches.

And, of course, the bishop's sermon was on sin and the evils of disobedience.

When the preaching was finally over, the bishop called Deacon Elias to the front of the barn. The two of them then called out Daniel for all he had done. Daniel didn't dare look up. His stomach was churning so badly, he could barely remain still and not double over. How in the world had his life come to this?

The deacon then asked Daniel to speak. Daniel's voice shook as he repented of his dealings with the *Englisch* newspaper and his indulgence in technology. And then came the lie.

"Daniel, you have also lied not only to me, but to the bishop. Do you repent of this?"

Daniel tried to swallow, but his throat was so dry and swollen that he was surprised to be still breathing. The silence in the barn was deafening. Even the children seemed to be holding their breath.

"I..." Daniel's voice faltered, but he pressed on. "I have not lied. I fully confess and repent of what I've done, but I have not lied."

A gasp from someone in the women's section could be clearly heard. Daniel knew it was his mother.

"So be it," Deacon Elias said. "I therefore suggest that Daniel Studer be silenced and that no one communicate with him until such a time as he repents."

Now, there was a low whisper of voices.

"We will vote," the bishop said, clearly in agreement.

At that point, the rest of the deacons came forward. Daniel knew what would happen next. They would walk through the people, leaning close to them to hear the *jah* or *nee* for the vote. Daniel's knees were shaking, but he remained standing. He wanted to sink onto the bench, but he couldn't do it. He didn't know if it was stubbornness or whether sinking onto the bench would be admitting his guilt, so he remained standing, praying fervently for strength.

There was a low rustle and whispered voices as the deacons circulated and heard the votes. Afterward, they gathered in the back before Deacon Elias came forward again.

"Daniel Studer is silenced until he repents and seeks forgiveness."

Daniel sucked in his breath. He'd known it would go that way, but hearing it took all the air from his body and dizziness filled him. He blinked and held on.

Church was dismissed and the women scattered to produce the community meal. The men began assembling the tables and rearranging the chairs. Daniel couldn't move. He knew he had to, for he was in the way. Finally, his legs worked again, and he walked out of the barn. The air hadn't warmed at all from earlier that morning. If anything, it felt colder than before.

It would take Daniel at least an hour to walk home, and so he set out down the drive. His parents would stay, showing their solidarity with the people, and Daniel wouldn't expect otherwise. He supposed he was lucky he hadn't been shunned.

How could this possibly end? The only way was if Daniel lied about telling the lie or Freddie came forward. As far as Daniel could foresee, he would be silenced forever. Tears burned in his eyes and he blinked them back.

Anna.

He needed to write to Anna.

～

THE BROKEN ENGAGEMENT

The house was still, and Daniel's footsteps echoed on the wooden floors in the front room. He went to the warming stove and bent down, mechanically throwing in another log. Then he moved to the bureau and found a tablet and a pen. He sat down on the davenport and began to write.

Dear Anna,

Thank you for telling me where you are. I'm so sorry that you're staying with your aenti. *I know she ain't your favorite person. I hope it's going all right.*

I was taken before the church today, as I'm sure you know. I have been silenced. Anna, Freddie denied everything. And when the bishop and Deacon Elias went to the police, there was no record of Freddie being arrested. He lied to me, Anna. Freddie lied.

And he won't admit it. He wouldn't even admit it to me when no one was listening. I don't know what to do. I don't want to confess to a lie I didn't tell. And I haven't lied, Anna. I've done wrong, but I haven't lied. Freddie won't even look at me now.

I think my parents believe me, but I don't know if they'll continue to believe me in the face of all this. I left right after the vote. There was no reason to stay as no one would speak to me, and I certainly couldn't eat with the folks.

Anna, forgive me. Please forgive me.

I hope to have better news the next time I write.

Daniel stopped writing. By saying there would be a next time, was he being presumptuous? Was he implying that Anna would certainly stay with him despite her father's edict? But he had to believe she would. He had to. For he suddenly felt as if everything had been stripped away from him.

No. That wasn't right. He'd done this to himself. Still, he had to believe that Anna would stick by him.

Another thought shook him. It wasn't fair, was it? To even hope she would? It wasn't fair to Anna. And how long would it take folks to figure out why she'd been sent away? Everyone would soon know or guess they had been engaged and now John Mast was against it.

With that in mind, he erased the last line and continued.

I hope that in time, you'll forgive the mess I made of things.

Daniel

His heart clenched as he wrote it. He hadn't even signed it *With love*. Anna would know what this meant—that he was backing away. Saying good-bye.

Maybe she'd write him back. Maybe she'd tell him they would make it through this. And if she did, it *would* be all right. She would be choosing him. He put the letter in the envelope, sealed it, and addressed it, praying fervently she would do just that.

Anna tread carefully in her aunt's house, and so far, it hadn't been as bad as she'd feared. It did help that Claire was more or less confined to the front room with her injured ankle. Anna wondered how Clair had managed without her help before she'd come. There was one good thing about it, and that was Claire certainly wouldn't be the one who gathered the mail each day. So, Anna would be able to intercept any mail meant for her.

Anna prayed for a letter from Daniel. She wanted so badly to know what had happened at preaching service. Monday brought no letter, but Tuesday, when she pried open the half-frozen mailbox, she saw her name on an envelope in Daniel's handwriting. She nearly gave a yelp of joy, snatching it to her heart and whispering a prayer of thanks. She gathered the other letters and hurried back up the drive to the house.

She gave Claire the other bits of mail and then disappeared upstairs. She closed her bedroom door and sat on the edge of her bed. The air in the room was frigid, but she didn't care. She ripped open Daniel's letter and began reading.

Her eyes grew wider and wider the further she read. How *dare* Freddie deny his part in things. How *dare* he accuse Daniel of lying. No longer able to sit still, she jumped up from her bed and began pacing. And now Daniel was silenced?

She stopped by the window and stared blindly outside. At least, he wasn't shunned, but wasn't being silenced almost as bad? *Ach,* poor Daniel.

Anna forced herself to finish the letter. When she read his last words and his closing, she stiffened. His whole tone had changed. Why had Daniel signed his letter with only his name? No words of endearment at all. He hadn't signed a letter to her like that in—well, *never.* What was he trying to tell her?

It was true she'd told him her father had stopped the engagement—was Daniel accepting that so easily? And if he was, how excited had he been to marry her in the first place? Confusion swirled through her. Was she so easy to give up?

She turned from the window and tossed his letter to the bed, hurt and perplexed.

When Luke had asked whether she was engaged or not, she had stammered and barely gotten an answer out. Well, it certainly seemed now that her wavering had been called for. It sounded like not only her father, but Daniel was putting an end to things.

Troubled, Anna left the room to go downstairs and work on supper.

Chapter Ten

Luke couldn't get Anna out of his head. At least, now he knew why she was there. His heart went out to her; this had to be hard. At the same time, he was thankful it had happened, or he might never have met her. And he was right glad they'd met. In just these few days, she had become a fixture in his mind. Never in his life had he thought about someone so constantly.

He found himself continually glancing toward Claire Mast's house when he was outside doing chores. He found himself thinking of excuses as to why he should go over there. Most of the excuses he thought up were ridiculous. But then, he thought of an excuse that just might not look so desperate.

He could go over and make sure there was enough chopped wood for the warming stoves. There was another cold snap expected in the next few days, and Claire might not be prepared for it. He didn't want Anna to have to go out in the cold and chop wood.

He went in search of his mother to let her know.

"*Mamm?*" he called.

"In here," she responded from the downstairs bedroom which she'd converted into a sewing room.

He popped his head into the room. "I thought I'd check to see if Claire has enough wood chopped for the cold spell we're expecting."

Lois's brow raised. "Oh?" she asked, and he could hear the teasing interest in her voice.

"It is supposed to get mighty cold."

"I don't doubt that. This winter has been harsh all around."

"Claire can't be out chopping wood with that ankle of hers."

"*Ach*, I hardly think so." Again, the teasing interest in her voice. "Of course, you might want to check *our* wood supply."

He frowned. "*Mamm*, you know full well that we—"

"And then, of course, we wouldn't want *Anna* to be out chopping wood, either, *ain't so?*"

Luke just stood there, looking at his mother.

Lois burst into laughter. "Luke Miller, if you could see the expression on your face..."

Luke had a pretty good idea about his expression right then. Naturally, his mother saw right through his flimsy excuse for going over to Claire's place.

"Fine," he said with exaggerated grumpiness, "you've figured it out."

Lois was smiling widely at him. "Anna Mast seems like a perfectly nice girl," she said. "I don't mind one bit if you want to get to know her better."

"I like her, *Mamm*."

"That's quite obvious. Well, don't let me get in your way." Lois picked up the shirt she was mending and took a stitch. "Get on over there. That wood ain't going to chop itself."

"I'll do that," Luke said, giving his mother a fond glance. The image of his father floated through his mind. It had been five years since cancer had taken him. He knew his mother still missed him; now and again, Luke heard her weeping at night. Soft-like, but he heard it. They'd had a good marriage; closer than a lot he'd observed. His dad had taken his mother's opinion into account, far more seriously than Luke saw in most relationships. And Luke had determined to do the same with his wife—when he had one. He understood the role of authority men played in his district, but he saw no problem with toning it down a bit. To his mind, it seemed excessive at times.

He left the house through the side door, deciding to walk over to Claire's as he and his mother had done the other day. It wasn't a long enough ride to hitch up the buggy or even the pony cart. He grinned—Claire's house's proximity made this only that much easier. He strode across the hard ground toward Claire's place. He was glad he'd grabbed his scarf; the air was bitter cold.

As he tromped across the barren corn field, he saw movement out by the barn. His heart beat a little faster. Was that Anna out there? Well, it could hardly be Claire, now, could it? He increased his pace. Was Anna seeing to the horse and the cow? If she was out in the barn, so much the better. They could chat a bit alone, which suited him fine.

He got to Claire's property and headed straight for the barn. The door was open, and he went in.

"Anna?" he asked as his eyes adjusted to the difference in light. After the bright light outside with the snow, the barn seemed to be shrouded in darkness.

"Luke? Is that you?" came her voice from the far corner.

His eyes adjusted now; he went to her. "Hello, Anna."

"What are you doing here?" she asked and then groaned. "*Ach,* but that sounded rude."

"No offense taken. Do you need help?"

"I'm about done out here. Thanks."

He patted Claire's milk cow on the flanks. "How you doin', girl?" He laughed. "Wouldn't we be surprised if she answered me. *Very gut, thank you most kindly.*" He intoned in what he hoped sounded like a cow's voice.

Anna stared at him and then burst out laughing. The sound filled him with such pleasure, he couldn't stop grinning.

"And just think," she surprised him by adding, "we could then put her in a circus and make bundles of money."

"We could have a whole routine for the beast," Luke said. "We could rehearse every Thursday morning at nine o'clock."

"Every Thursday..." Anna repeated, amused. "Why ... *jah,* I think every Thursday morning is perfect. I'll clear my schedule."

Luke gazed at her, wondering at how such a delightful creature could exist. No wonder she was already engaged. But, no more. Right? Wasn't that what she'd told him? So, he was free to court her, and oh, how he wanted to court her.

"But really," she said, "did you need something?"

"I'm here to check on your wood supply. We're in for a cold snap, and I don't want you—I mean, I don't want either *Claire* or you running out of wood for your warming stove."

He couldn't be sure, but he thought he saw Anna's eyes mist over at his words. But just as quickly, it was gone, and she smiled at him.

"That's right neighborly of you. I think there's plenty. It's around the side of the house, if you want to check."

"I do want to check." He hesitated. "You about ready? We can go back up to the house together."

"Did you walk over?"

"I did."

She didn't say anything to that, but she fastened the stall door, and they set out toward the house. The walked together in companionable silence, Luke's mind so full of Anna's sweetness and charm that he was surprised she couldn't hear his thoughts. Around the side of the house, she showed him the woodpile. In truth, there was ample wood for the rest of the winter. He was almost disappointed, wanting to do something for both her and Claire.

"Looks like you're set," he said.

"*Jah,* I think Claire had it sorted before winter started. She's very organized."

He laughed. "That she is."

"Thank you for coming, though," Anna continued, her voice soft. "It was kind of you to worry about me, I mean, about Claire and me."

He stared into her eyes, and he couldn't stop himself from saying, "You had it right the first time, Anna."

And with that, he turned and walked away.

Chapter Eleven

Anna sucked in her breath and watched him leave. She watched the easy way he walked, as if he hadn't a care in the world. As if he knew his place in life and was well content. Though he wasn't a big man, his shoulders were broad. Anna could sense his strength, and she knew his good nature. Whenever he was around, she felt better somehow. As if the world were a better place.

She shivered, and she wasn't sure it was from the cold. Was she falling for him? She feared she was, and it gave her a horrible sinking feeling. She felt as if she were betraying Daniel, for hadn't she so recently promised to marry him? And now, here she stood, enthralled with another...

She thought again of Daniel's letter. It had felt like a dismissal. A stark ending to their relationship. But maybe she was mistaken. He was upset. Of *course*, he was upset, and maybe he hadn't written things the way he really meant them. But oh, it had felt like he was cutting her off. She thought of how stern and disapproving her father had looked when he'd told her she was no longer engaged.

She let out her breath in a puff of white steam. For just an instant, she wondered at how *Englisch* girls handled such things. She had a feeling they didn't have to obey their fathers in affairs of the heart. Particularly when they were over eighteen years old.

But she wasn't *Englisch*, was she?

She had an obligation to obey her father. For that was *Gott's* will for her.

Wasn't it?

Anna shook her head and turned to go back into the house. She was shivering now, and she figured it was also time to get her aunt a cup of tea. Claire liked to have tea regularly throughout the day, and she seemed quite happy now that Anna was there to serve her. Anna was glad for it; being useful eased the tension between them. Tension that was always present with Claire, as far as Anna was concerned. The woman found fault with nearly everything.

But she did like the way Anna made tea.

Anna went in through the side door and slipped out of her heavy black shoes. She took off her coat and her scarf and hung them on the waiting peg. She pulled off her gloves and set them on the bench. Then she went into the kitchen and turned on a burner of the cook stove. She filled the kettle with water and set it on the burner.

"Anna!" came Claire's strident voice.

Anna hurried into the front room. "*Jah, Aenti?*"

"Did I hear someone?"

Anna's eyes widened slightly. How in the world had Claire heard Luke from the front room? Truly, the woman's ears were beyond human capacity.

"Luke stopped by."

"Why didn't you ask him in for tea? What did he want?"

"He was checking to see if we had enough wood with the coming cold spell."

"The coming..." And then a look of satisfaction covered her face. She nodded to herself and gave a half-smile. "Oh, he did, did he?"

Anna studied her aunt's face.

Claire went on. "He's a *gut* lad, is Luke Miller. *Gut* mother, too. Such a shame about his *dat*."

Anna was eager to know what had happened to Luke's father, but she wasn't sure she wanted to hear it from Claire. She wasn't sure she wanted to talk to Claire about Luke at all—particularly in light of the self-satisfied look covering her aunt's face. As if she'd just accomplished something lovely.

"I've put the kettle on," Anna said.

Claire gave her a sharp look. "Don't try to change the subject."

Anna's mouth opened to protest, but she closed it just as fast.

"I think we'll be having Luke and his *mamm* for a noon meal. How about tomorrow? *Jah,* tomorrow would suit. You'll have to be going over there to invite them." She craned her neck, peering past Anna out the window. "Don't look like it's going to snow again right away. Bundle up, girl, and get on over there. If you're quick about it, you might catch Luke before he gets home."

"But *Aenti,* I've put the kettle on."

"And you can take it off. Get going, girl."

Anna hurried from the room. She should be annoyed with the way Claire was ordering her about, but to her surprise, she wasn't. As she turned off the burner, she realized she was smiling. And that realization filled her with guilt.

What was the matter with her? She was completely out of control.

Poor Daniel was dealing with heartbreak and discipline and not being believed by his own family, and she was excited about sharing a meal with another man.

"Hurry up!" came her aunt's voice.

Anna quickly went to the washroom and bundled up again. She dashed outside and half-ran down the drive. She didn't dare go any faster than that, as there were ice patches scattered about, some quite disguised on the gravel drive. When she reached the road, she realized that she should have simply tromped across the field to the Miller farm like Luke had, but it was too late now. She wouldn't catch Luke on his way now, anyway, for he'd probably had enough time to make it home.

Well, there was nothing for it now but to go along the road. She walked well to the side in case any cars came by, but all was quiet. There was the echoing hush of impending snowfall, and despite the cold, she found it quite peaceful and calming as she slowed her pace. Her mind slowed down, too, along with her feet.

THE BROKEN ENGAGEMENT

Perhaps she shouldn't be so hard on herself. Some things simply weren't under her control. She used to rebel against that—if only quietly, but she found it never helped. Indeed, trying to take control of some things only resulted in heartache and frustration. So now, she took a deep breath of the frigid air and prayed.

Dear Gott, I don't know what is going on right now. I feel quite confused. I do know that I was sent here to get me away from Daniel, and I didn't like that. I still don't. But now... I just don't know. Perhaps it was wise to get out of Hollybrook for a time. Was this truly from You? Me here? Me meeting Luke Miller? I don't know what to think right now.

A blackbird flew from a nearby tree across the sky. It soared against the gray looking so free. She watched it until it alighted on another tree, perching on a naked branch. What must it feel like to fly like that? It must feel so wonderful—so unbound. She scoffed lightly at such a frivolous idea.

Maybe she was just thinking too much. Did she have to analyze every single thought that went through her head? Did other people do that? She had no idea, but it was wearying, that was for sure and for certain. She focused on the ground ahead, noting the scattered stalks of weeds, standing frozen and forlorn.

The Miller's drive wasn't too far ahead. Her pulse quickened as she imagined Luke's surprise at seeing her again, and so soon. Her pace increased as a gust of wind blew into her face. She was shivering when she reached the drive. She'd hoped Luke would still be outside so she wouldn't have to go to the door, but no such luck. She couldn't see him anywhere.

She went to the house, climbed the porch steps and knocked on the door. It opened immediately to Luke's surprised expression.

"Anna," he cried. "Come in. Come in. Has something happened?"

Why must he be so kind? And why must her eyes always mist over in the face of it.

"*Nee, nee,*" she said quickly. "I've come with an invitation for you and your *mamm* from *Aenti* Claire."

His brow raised, and he stepped back. "Then, shall we go see *Mamm?*"

She followed him into the kitchen where his mother was putting dishes away. "Why, Anna, how nice to see you again," she said. "Take off your coat and sit down, child. You must be half-frozen."

Anna couldn't understand why other adults kept calling her child, for she hardly was one. At twenty-six, she was practically an old *maidel*. But she did as she was bidden. Luke's mother's voice was so welcoming and warm, that she felt right at home—more so than she felt at her aunt's place.

Lois Miller moved to the cook stove and took the kettle off. She then began arranging cups and saucers and tea, bringing Anna a steaming cup within no more than a minute or two. Luke sat across from her, taking a cup of tea from his mother, too.

Finally, Lois sat down with them. "So nice of you to stop by, Anna. How's Claire?"

"She's doing fine," Anna said. "I've come to invite you and Luke to Claire's tomorrow for the noon meal."

"Why, ain't that nice?" Lois said, glancing at Luke. "We will surely be there. You are free, Luke, *ain't so?*"

Luke gave his mother a knowing look, although Anna couldn't quite figure out what he was saying silently to his mother. Then he looked at Anna. "We'd be delighted to come."

"*Gut.* I'll tell *Aenti.*"

"How are you liking it here in Linder Creek?" Lois asked. "It sure is nice that you're here for a spell."

"I'm liking it fine," Anna said. "Although in truth, I haven't seen much more than the inside of my *aenti's* house?"

"And the mercantile, *ain't so?*" Luke smiled at her.

"*Jah,* that's true."

"Well, we must do something about that," Lois said. "Perhaps Luke can take you around a bit one of these days."

Anna felt the heat creep up her neck. It was quite clear what Lois was doing, and she didn't dare look at Luke to see his reaction, but then he burst out laughing, his guffaws filling the room.

"*Ach, Mamm,* could you be more obvious?"

Lois didn't look the least chagrinned. "If not, I'm certainly obvious now," she said drily.

Luke kept laughing. "*Mamm,* you are wonderful."

Anna barely kept herself from gaping at them. Their relationship—the way they joked with each other—was so foreign to her. It gave her a strange yearning deep in her heart; an empty feeling which was so strange. Then Luke turned to her with that warm open smile of his and something in her rose up to meet him.

She felt her cheeks color and she quickly looked down at her tea, inspecting it as if it were the most interesting thing she'd ever seen.

"All that to say, we will be there," Luke said. She glanced up at him now and something in his eyes seemed to indicate that he understood her longing. She blinked, but she didn't look away.

"*Ach*, I've left something in the front room," Lois said, setting her tea down and rising to her feet. "Please excuse me."

After she left the room, Luke leaned slightly across the table. "Anna, this is our cue."

"What? What do you mean?"

"My *mamm* has conveniently left the room so you and I can get to know each other. Shall we accommodate her?"

"What do you mean?" Anna couldn't figure this man out, but she found herself totally intrigued.

His tone turned conspiratorial. "Let's laugh and laugh and laugh, pretending I just told a charming joke. She'll be dying of curiosity."

Anna's mouth fell open. And then he started to laugh, and it was so contagious that she couldn't help but join in. Before she knew it, they were doing just as Luke had suggested.

He finally stopped laughing long enough to say, "I love to hear you laugh."

She grew silent and looked at him. The atmosphere in the room shifted, and a feeling of intimacy filled the air. She tried to look away, but she found her gaze locked onto his as if she had no will of her own. His smile deepened, and he reached across the table and touched her hand. The contact zapped through her.

"You make spring seem a whole lot closer," he said, and then he blanched slightly as if shocked by what had come out of his mouth.

"S-spring?" she said, her voice low.

He laughed again, but this time it seemed a bit nervous and uncomfortable.

She licked her lips and then stood. "I should be getting back."

"I'll walk you."

"*Nee,* you don't have to do that," she protested.

"I know I don't, but I'm going to do it just the same." He stood and picked up both their cups and saucers and carried them to the counter.

Anna stared at him, still unused to seeing a man being helpful in the kitchen.

"I'll just tell *Mamm,* and then we'll be on our way."

"All right," Anna said. It was like she'd walked into another world in the Miller house. She was awed by it—by the light mood, the spirited banter, the mutual helpfulness. It wasn't that those things were never present in her own home back in Hollybrook, but they weren't so obvious nor so prevalent. Not that she'd had much experience in Luke's household, but still... She pushed in the bench she'd been sitting on and realized she wanted to stay.

And not only right that minute, but for a long, long time. The realization smacked her hard and she faltered. Just then Luke reappeared.

"You ready?" he asked. His smile faded. "What's wrong?"

She sucked in a breath. "Nothing. Nothing is wrong." She put on a smile. "Shall we go?"

He held out her coat to her. She took it quickly and put it on, along with her gloves and scarf. He'd already put his own coat on.

"Let's go brave the wild frontier, shall we?"

Her smile turned genuine now. "The wild frontier? *Jah,* let's."

They took off through the washroom and the side door. "We'll cut across the fields," Luke said. "Is that the way you came over?"

"*Nee.* I didn't think of it until it was too late."

"Come on." And now he increased his pace until he was half-running. She laughed and caught up to him. He slowed, and they resumed walking.

Anna's cheeks were cold, and the dry air burned at her eyes, but she'd never felt so invigorated.

"Anna?"

"*Jah?*"

"I'd like to take you riding. We can go in the afternoon instead of the evening if you like. That way you could see some of Linder Creek."

She bit her lip. Dare she agree? She wanted to.

Ach, she needed to talk to Daniel. She needed to know what was going on. It was true that she wasn't engaged anymore, but did that mean she didn't have a beau anymore, too?

"I-I..." she stammered. "I need to do some things first."

He stopped walking and so did she. "It's all right," he said, his eyes intense on hers. "I know things are complicated."

She nodded, grateful he understood.

"But, Anna, there is something you need to know."

She held her breath, giving him a questioning look.

"I'm fond of you." He moved his eyebrows up and down and grinned. "I'm thinking more than fond, and I'd like to find out. So, I will ask again."

Her heart was hammering. How was it possible to feel this close to someone she just met? How was it possible to be drawn to someone when she'd already pledged her heart to someone else?

"Let's go," he said suddenly, tugging on her coat sleeve. They half-ran, half-skipped across the remainder of the field until they stood, breathless, at the foot of Claire's porch stairs.

"Thank you for walking me home..." She laughed. "I mean for running me home."

He joined her laughter. "You're most welcome. *Mamm* and I will see you tomorrow."

He walked back down the sidewalk and then paused, turning back. "*Gut*-bye, Anna."

She warmed at how her name sounded on his tongue. And the look he gave her took her breath away. She stood watching as he turned back around and left, cutting through the grass to the field. She wrapped her arms around herself, and then the thrill of her feelings gave her pause.

She turned and walked into the house to write a letter to Daniel.

Chapter Twelve

Daniel went about his chores, wishing he had more to do. It was still winter, and his list of chores was woefully inadequate to take his mind off things. He felt as good as shunned. No one would speak to him or look at him—not that he'd given anyone much of a chance. He'd pretty much holed up at the farm, praying this would soon be over. With every day that passed, he bemoaned his stupidity for agreeing to write for that online paper. With that decision, he had effectively destroyed his life.

But he'd done it for Freddie—thinking it was vital and necessary.

Yet if he faced it again, he'd never agree to it. He should never have compromised himself no matter what his reason. And now Freddie was being a complete liar and fraud, and Daniel was the one being punished for it. He thought of Anna, stuck in Linder Creek because of him. He squeezed his eyes shut and let out his breath in a heavy sigh. Anna. She was lost to him now, too.

THE BROKEN ENGAGEMENT

He shouldn't give up so easily, should he? But the heaviness of her father's displeasure sat on his shoulders like bags of wet cement. He'd been cold to her in his last letter. He'd basically cut her off. Had she taken it that way? He'd felt obliged to do it. How could he expect to keep her by his side amidst her own father's prohibition and the district's silencing? It would make him feel even worse.

Resigned to his fate, he picked up the pitchfork and tossed a forkful of hay into the horse's stall.

Anna saw to Claire, making sure she had everything she needed, and then she went upstairs to her room. She didn't bother shutting her door as she was certain Claire wouldn't be venturing up the stairs with her hurt ankle. Anna's room was austere, having only a bed, a dresser, a nightstand, and some pegs on the wall. It was painted a beige color and the curtains that hung at the window were also beige. The only spot of brightness and color was the impeccably made quilt of blue and yellow. The pattern was a familiar one—Anna had made the same pattern with her mother two years before. But not as fine as this one. These stitches were small and precise. If Anna didn't know better, she'd think it was made by a machine.

But, of course, it was made by Claire.

Anna sat on it almost reverently. But once she got out her tablet and pen, all thoughts of the quilt and its perfection flew out of her head. She had to write to Daniel. She had to find out if he indeed had called their relationship off. She truly didn't know how she felt about it anymore. Her feelings had become a jumbled mess.

She took a deep breath and began to write.

Dear Daniel,

I'm pained you were silenced. I imagine it is devastating for you. I can hardly believe Freddie has denied his part in things. That must hurt most of all. I confess that it makes me feel angry toward Freddie. I am praying about my anger as I'm certain it isn't pleasing to Gott.

Daniel, I need to know something. Perhaps this is quite forward of me, but I must ask. I got the feeling you were calling things off between us. I need to know. If you could please explain, I would be grateful.

I am praying for you.

Anna

Anna let out her breath and read over what she'd written. It was short and to the point. She stared at her name at the end. She hadn't put anything besides her name, the same way Daniel hadn't put anything besides his name in his last letter. It felt strange not to put "All my love" like she always did. But she didn't want to keep something going that was over.

Her thoughts went to Luke—she didn't want to be thinking of him; she truly didn't. But her mind went there all the same. She sighed heavily. The truth of it was hard to avoid. She had to face up to the fact that one of the reasons she'd written Daniel was because of Luke. She wanted to know if she was free.

She licked her lips. Free? She wasn't sure what that meant. Was a person ever truly free to pursue what they wanted? In her life, she hadn't found it so. There were so many rules and expectations, that conforming properly was never far from her mind.

Yet, no one was forcing her to remain with Daniel. In fact, it was just the opposite. But she wanted to be fair. She wanted to be kind. She wanted to do the right thing.

But wait...

If she truly loved Daniel in the way she thought she did, then nothing could get in the way of it. Not in her heart, anyway. But something had gotten in the way. Something had caused her to doubt her feelings for Daniel.

Luke Miller.

With determination, Anna folded up her letter to Daniel and stuck it in an envelope. She addressed it, stuck a stamp on it and then left her room to grab her coat downstairs and run out to the mailbox. As she breathed in the crisp air and felt the mist of shimmering ice, she determined something else.

She had to ignore her growing feelings for Luke Miller. Until she knew for sure what Daniel was thinking, it was wrong to give Luke a moment's thought.

Daniel's breath caught as he stared at the envelope in his family's mailbox. There was no mistaking the handwriting. He snatched it up and stood there at the end of the drive and ripped it open. He quickly read Anna's words, his eyes settling on her closing. *Anna.* That was all. He drew in a shaky breath.

In truth, he wasn't surprised. His last letter had shaken her; that was clear. Well, what had he expected? He read her letter again, imagining her expressions and feelings as she wrote it. His forehead scrunched in concentration, and he read it through for the third time. There was something there.

Something had changed.

He blew out his breath. He was losing her—or he'd already lost her. He heard it in the words she hadn't said. She was waiting for his confirmation. She wanted him to tell her it was over.

He reached out and grabbed the cold metal mailbox for support as his knees went weak. Anna *wanted* it to be over. She hadn't said so—not directly. But he knew her; he knew her so well. And she was finished with him.

His eyes welled with tears. This was his doing; he could hardly fault Anna. He let go of the mailbox and squared his shoulders. Someday, this whole nightmare would pass, and his silencing would be over. He had no idea how or when, but he felt an odd sense of sudden surety that it would happen. But even so—afterward—things would never be quite the same for him.

He would never be looked upon in the same way. Even as his spirit recoiled at this idea, he knew it to be true. He would always be the one who had been silenced; the one who wouldn't repent—despite the fact that he hadn't lied. Still, he'd done enough, hadn't he? That mark would always be on him. Forgiveness or not.

And he didn't want that for Anna. He didn't. He wanted her to be free. It wasn't right to drag her down with him. Setting Anna free was something he *could* do. Something noble and kind and loving. Something that would help him regain his lost sense of personal dignity. Something he could sacrifice that would help restore his pride. Not the arrogant conceited pride the Bible warned against, but the basic pride of knowing he was a decent person who did decent things.

He blinked back his tears and the knots in his stomach loosened. He began to feel good about himself for the first time in weeks. Maybe in months.

He would do this for Anna and in that way, for himself. He grabbed the rest of the mail and went inside.

The next day, Claire had Anna in the kitchen early. Luke and his mother were coming that day for the noon meal, and Claire wanted everything perfect. She had made her way to the kitchen and set herself up at the kitchen table, with her bad foot propped on the bench. From there, she reigned, bossing Anna about as if Anna hadn't a clue how to cook a meal.

Anna was ready to hide herself in a closet by the time the noon hour approached. Claire was making her beyond nervous. But she had to admit, the meal of roast, potatoes and carrots, gravy, green beans, salad, and a fresh cherry pie—from Claire's canned cherries the summer before—was perfection itself. The smells from the kitchen had permeated the house, and Anna found herself not only gratified but starving.

Claire had her set the dining table and put out her best cloth napkins.

"Get on upstairs and fix yourself," Claire admonished at the last moment. "A fresh dress wouldn't go amiss."

"But *Aenti*... They'll be here any moment."

"So get on with you," Claire said impatiently. "I won't have Luke seeing you in such a state."

Anna reached up to smooth her hair under her *kapp*. It didn't feel such a mess. She glanced down at her apron. It could stand changing; there were a few splatters here and there.

"Go on," Claire urged.

Anna left the room and took the stairs two at a time to her room. She saw her tablet and pen resting on the dresser, and her mind flew to Daniel. Had he gotten her letter yet? It shouldn't take more than a day to get there. But then, his mail, like her family's, was delivered later in the afternoon. So no, he wouldn't have gotten it yet. She bit the corner of her lip, wishing she could just talk to him face-to-face. Letters were a good substitute, but nothing was as good as being present with a person.

She heard someone knocking at the door downstairs. *Ach,* they were here. She threw off her apron and ran downstairs without putting on a fresh one. She didn't want Claire to have to make her way to answer the door.

"I'll get it," she called out and rushed to the door, throwing it open.

Luke and Lois Miller stood there, smiling at her. Lois had a jar of what looked to be blackberry jam in her hands.

"Come in, come in," Anna said, standing back.

"This is for you and Claire," Lois said, holding out the jam.

"How lovely," Anna murmured, trying to still her racing heart as she took the jar. Luke was studying her, and it unnerved her.

"Have you been running?" Luke asked, his eyes twinkling with mischief. "Excited to get to the door—"

"Luke Miller," his mother scolded, although she didn't look in the least perturbed. "Mind your manners."

"*Jah, Mamm.* You know I will."

Lois chuckled and swept past Anna toward the kitchen. "Hello, Claire. You're looking downright perky today."

Since Claire was still in the kitchen, Anna couldn't make out how she replied. She herself was too busy trying to evade Luke. Which was hopeless. His gaze caught hers, and she couldn't have moved away if she'd tried.

"How are you, Anna?" This time, his voice was low and resonant and somehow intimate, even though his mother and her aunt were only a stone's throw away.

"I-I'm fine," she stammered, closing the front door.

"It smells right *gut* in here," he said, sniffing appreciatively.

"Thank you."

"And I'm right hungry." He laughed.

"Claire had me make enough to feed the whole church," Anna said, smiling now, and feeling a bit more balanced. "Come on through to the dining room."

He followed her, too closely, she thought. She caught the scent of him—the outdoors, the straw, and a touch of something else—the trees maybe.

Fanciful, she thought to herself.

"Hello, Luke," Claire said. She'd come out to the dining room from the kitchen. She was now sitting in her chair at the head of the table, and Lois was standing beside her. "I hope you're *gut* and hungry."

Lois laughed heartily. "That's never a problem with our Luke.".

"*Mamm's* right," Luke agreed. "Truly, *Mamm* spends her whole life bustling about the kitchen feeding me."

Lois stepped over and gave Luke a tender slap on the shoulder. "*Ach,* how you go on."

"Anna, bring out the meal, will you?" Claire said. "Lois, Luke, please feel free to sit down."

Anna went into the kitchen. She opened the oven and took out the large roaster pan. She set it on the cutting board on the counter and turned to the fridge, nearly knocking into Luke.

"*Ach,* Luke!"

"I thought I'd help you carry the meal in," he said. "What would you like me to take?"

The man continually surprised her. She didn't think she'd ever seen her father carry one bowl of food from the kitchen to the table in her entire life.

"Um… You can get the salad out of the refrigerator," she said. "I'll just put the green beans into a bowl."

Together, they got the steaming meal onto the table. Claire asked Luke to lead the silent blessing, and then they all dug in. Anna's nerves were jumping about, but even so, she managed to enjoy the meal. Luke had a way of making everything entertaining. Before long, all four of them were talking and laughing and having a nice time.

Lois helped Anna clear the table and *red* up the kitchen. Despite her thinly veiled pressure about Luke taking her about Linder Creek, Anna enjoyed her time with Lois. She could see where Luke got his joy of life.

"I think even Claire would approve of this kitchen now," Lois said, putting her hands on her hips and surveying the sparkling kitchen.

Anna laughed. "That she would."

"Shall we go out and join her and Luke?"

Anna nodded and they went out to the front room together. They chatted a bit more and then Lois stood and said, "Luke, we must get going."

Luke stood. "I s'pose so. I do hate to leave our charming hostesses, however."

Ach, but the things the man said.

"Don't be a stranger," Claire said, looking inordinately pleased with herself. "And Luke, I'm thinking maybe you could take Anna to the livery and see about the bridle Josh is repairing."

"*Aenti,* I'm sure Luke doesn't—" Anna started, but Luke cut her off.

"That's a right *gut* idea. I'll take her tomorrow. *Mamm* was thinking I should show Anna around Linder Creek a bit, anyway."

"It's settled then," Claire said, folding her hands on her lap and smiling.

Anna took a deep breath. She wasn't too thrilled with how all these decisions were being made on her behalf. Luke glanced at her and seemed to know what she was thinking.

"That is, if it's all right with you, Anna." His gaze rested gently on her.

"I-I..." She hesitated and then realized that, of course, she wanted him to take her to the livery the next day. And the day after that. And the day after that. She slumped slightly, giving up. "*Jah*, that would be nice. Thank you."

"We'll be going then. Thank you kindly for the lovely meal. Anna, you're a fine cook," Lois said.

Anna felt her cheeks warm. Before she could say anything, Luke and Lois were putting on their heavy coats. She hurried to open the front door for them.

"Tomorrow around two? Would that suit?" Luke asked her.

"That will suit," she said, suddenly feeling shy.

"*Gut*-bye," Lois said. She reached over and squeezed Anna's arm and then she was out the door, Luke following her.

Chapter Thirteen

Dear Anna, Daniel started. He inhaled deeply and kept writing...

I got your letter. I understand your confusion, and I am right sorry for that. I wasn't clear. Indeed, I don't think I was clear in my own mind, so I wasn't able to be clear with you.

But there is a clarity now to my thinking. And you're right. I am calling it off between us. It is only proper considering the situation I'm in. I want you to know that I wish you all the best. The very, very best for your future.

I do hope we can be friends. Right now, that would be impossible, of course. You're not here, and even if you were, we wouldn't be in contact. But later, when this is all over, I hope we can be friends.

Thank you, Anna. Thank you. I'm so sorry things had to end this way. Deeply sorry.

Daniel

. . .

Daniel dropped his pen and sank back against the headboard of his bed. There. It was done. With this letter, it was all over. He felt a mixture of heartache and relief. And deep, deep sorrow. A sorrow that sank into him and spread through him like a wave of tears. He had planned to marry Anna and have a family with her. He had planned to be with Anna until the day he died. He hadn't come to the decision to marry her lightly, nor had he come to this decision to call it off lightly. It had cost him.

Cost him dearly.

But his grief was tempered with a growing sense of integrity. He was taking charge of his life and his actions, and that felt good and right. In time, he felt sure that the truth of Freddie would come out. And then, Daniel would be welcomed back.

Welcomed back without Anna at his side.

So be it. This was the decision he had made.

It turned out that Anna didn't go to the livery with Luke the next day. Lois had unexpectedly needed the buggy and horse, so they had made arrangements to go the following day. Anna woke up that morning with a strange feeling in her stomach. Something was going to happen that day; she could sense it. Was something going to happen between her and Luke?

She was determined that it would not. She hadn't yet heard back from Daniel.

Wait... Was that what was going to happen? Would she receive a letter from him that day? The hours of the morning inched by in nervous bursts. Anna could barely concentrate on the bread she was making. Nor could she concentrate on the set of linen curtains Claire had asked her to hem.

Every hour, she ran out to the mailbox checking for Daniel's letter.

By the time noon came around, she could hardly contain herself. Claire had hobbled into the kitchen and was sitting at the kitchen table.

"*Ach,* what ails you, child? You're so jittery. You're making me nervous. What is it?"

She could hardly tell Claire she was awaiting a letter from Daniel. If Claire knew they were still communicating, her ire would know no bounds. And then she'd contact Anna's father, and the sparks would really fly.

She swallowed and said, "I'm thinking about my ride with Luke later."

She felt totally guilty for lying, but she knew it would satisfy Claire. And it did. Claire gave her a gentle smile. "You'll have a right *gut* time, Anna. You know what a fine man Luke is."

And Anna did know. She supposed that maybe her comment hadn't been a total lie. True, she was mostly nervous about what Daniel would say, but the fact she'd be spending the afternoon with Luke hadn't escaped her notice—or her nerves, either.

She glanced out the kitchen window in time to glimpse the mail truck pulling away from the end of their drive.

"*Aenti,* the mail has come. Why don't I dash out to get it for you?"

"That'd be right nice. Bundle up."

Anna put down the dishtowel she was holding and went into the washroom. She grabbed her coat, pulling it on quickly as she went out the side door. She hurried down the drive. Her aunt wouldn't stand up from the table, as that was still somewhat of an ordeal for her, so she wouldn't be watching Anna retrieve the mail. Anna could pause out there and read Daniel's letter.

For she was now sure there would be a letter from him in today's mail. She simply knew it. Her pace increased to the mailbox; although, she was careful not to slip on the erratic patches of ice scattered here and there. She pulled open the tiny metal door of the mailbox and reached inside. Her breath caught.

There it was. On top. Just as she'd known it would be.

She glanced toward the house and of course didn't see Claire peering out the window. Anna turned her back to the house and with shaking fingers, ripped open the letter. She took the short message in with her breath still held. And then she began trembling all over.

He had done it. He had broken their relationship.

He had *done* it.

She was breathing erratically now as she crammed his letter into her coat pocket. She grasped the rest of the mail to her chest and began slowly walking back to the house.

She and Daniel were over. He had decided not to fight for her.

She blinked back sudden tears. Why hadn't he tried harder?

No. She couldn't go there. What good would it do? He had made his decision. He had decided they were over.

Somewhere in the deepest recesses of her heart, Anna knew he saw this decision as a loving act. Because he was that way... He wouldn't want her to be involved in the mess he was in. He was a good, kind, loving person.

Just not *her* person. Not anymore.

She trudged up the drive. Was she relieved? She had to admit that part of her was. For she hadn't felt the same about Daniel since his revelation. She wanted someone who would consider her when making his decisions. She wanted someone who would cherish her and their future above all else but God.

But another part grieved. *Ach,* Daniel. This wasn't how she'd hoped it would be.

She hesitated outside the side door and took a deep breath. This meant, of course, that she was free to be courted. And Luke wanted to court her—he'd been surprisingly frank about that. And she did like him. She liked the way she felt when she was around him. She liked being with him. Listening to him. Laughing with him.

Did that make her a terrible person?

Because she had feelings for another man so soon? Maybe it did. But there it was. She liked Luke, and despite everything, she was glad she would be spending the afternoon with him.

She went into the house, shed her coat and shoes, and padded into the kitchen. She handed Claire the rest of the mail.

"Thank you, child," Claire said. Her eyes narrowed. "What's the matter?"

Anna gave a start. "What? What do you mean?"

"You look odd." Her brow rose. "Did you get a letter?"

"Wh-why would you ask that? I just got a letter from my folks the other day. Even my sister Prudence doesn't write that often." Anna forced her expression to remain relaxed and open.

Claire stared at her for another long moment and then sighed. "Suit yourself," she said.

Anna swallowed. "Umm, I'm going to switch out my *kapp* before Luke gets here."

"Aren't you forgetting something? We haven't eaten the noon meal yet."

Anna stopped short. What in the world was she thinking? "*Ach*, of course. I don't know where my mind is. I guess I'm a bit nervous."

And then Claire chuckled, and Anna knew she was safe.

"Well, you need to eat something before you go," Claire said. "Bring over that pot of stew you've been simmering for hours. You can have a bowl of that. Then, you can switch out your *kapp*."

Luke whistled as he hitched up the buggy to pick up Anna. He was excited—there were no two ways about it. He knew Anna had been a bit coerced into agreeing to go with him, but he was glad anyway. He wasn't choosy about how he was able to see her.

He just wanted to see her.

He was grinning widely now, imagining her sitting beside him in the buggy. If he had his way, it would be a common—if not permanent—situation. Strange how he was so certain of his feelings toward her. After all the pressure from his mother over the last couple years, he'd finally fallen for someone.

If only Anna didn't have such a complicated situation right then. But still, the other day he had seen something in her eyes. Something that hinted at her own feelings for him, and he was going to focus on that. He didn't want to be too early. But he'd checked the clock in the kitchen before coming outside, so by now, he figured it was all right for him to head straight over there.

He'd already bid his mother farewell, so he was ready to go. He glanced across the field toward Claire's place, but he saw no movement. Anna was surely inside, hopefully waiting eagerly for him.

Chapter Fourteen

Anna stood by the front window, waiting. Claire was watching her, so she tried not to look too eager or too nervous or too anything. Claire unnerved her sometimes, and this was one of those times. She knew Claire wanted nothing more than for her to fall for Luke Miller. If Claire had her way, Anna would marry him. Anna wasn't sure if Claire's motivation was because she saw them as a good match, or whether she just wanted to show Anna's father that she had fixed the whole situation of his daughter for him.

But whatever the reason, Claire's gaze boring holes in her back was disturbing to say the least. When Luke finally pulled up in his buggy, Anna didn't wait for him to come to the door. She just tossed a good-bye to her aunt over her shoulder and hurried outside.

"Hello, Anna," Luke greeted her. He'd leaned over and opened her door for her. He sat in the driver's seat with a wide, welcoming smile.

THE BROKEN ENGAGEMENT

"Hello, Luke." She climbed into the buggy and sat beside him. *Ach,* but she'd never noticed much before just how narrow a buggy was. She'd sat beside Daniel plenty of times, but she'd never felt so ... so *close* to him. Now she felt almost as if she were sitting practically on Luke's lap. Which, of course, was ridiculous.

"We'll stop by the livery first, all right? Then we can drive around as much as we wish, and I will show you the thoroughly exciting places in Linder Creek. Why we have a thrilling one-room schoolhouse, a delicious mouth-watering bakery, a library chock full of fascinating volumes, a..." He paused and then laughed. "I'm running out of descriptions."

She laughed with him, marveling again at how quickly life became fun and pleasant and, well, happier in Luke's presence. She wasn't so foolish as to think that Luke's life was always perfectly happy, but she knew his attitude would make an enormous difference in whatever he faced. It was an intriguing thought.

"I s'pose if you're ever in Hollybrook, I can return the favor." The minute she said the words, she felt her face color. Would she truly go with him around Hollybrook, pointing out all the sites? Didn't that imply a continuing relationship?

Would Luke think she was telling him something she wasn't?

She glanced over at him. He was looking at her, his eyes bright and merry, so yes, he was reading into her comment. She was about to set him straight when she stopped herself. Wasn't she telling the truth now? Hadn't she decided to get to know him better the moment Daniel told her it was over?

She hadn't admitted it so clearly and boldly to herself, but that was exactly what she'd been thinking.

"I think that's a fine idea," Luke said. He reached over and touched her sleeve briefly. "I'd like to see where you grew up. Not that I haven't been to Hollybrook before. Well, more like gone through Hollybrook before. I don't really know it."

Her heart was beating wildly now as she thought about Luke in Hollybrook. She did want him to see where she grew up. She did want to show him around the places that meant so much to her, but she didn't say anything further. Daniel's image was stuck in her mind, and she felt guilt tugging at her heart.

Luke was watching her, and his gaze turned gentle and soft. "It's all right," he said. "Whatever it is you're worried about. It's all right."

How did he know? And how did he know she was suddenly feeling off? It was uncanny how the man could read her.

"I..." She sucked in a huge breath and continued. "I ... heard from Daniel."

His eyes widened, but other than that, there was no reaction. His gaze remained steady on her.

"He... He has broken it off." She pressed her lips together and was embarrassed to realize her eyes had filled with tears.

His brow furrowed slightly. "I imagine that was painful."

She let out her breath. "*Jah. Jah*, it was," she said, her words rushing forward. And then she clapped a hand over her mouth. Why in the world was she sharing her pain with him? She didn't know him that well.

He touched her sleeve again, this time letting his hand rest there for a longer moment. He smiled at her and then turned his focus back to the road. She got the distinct feeling he understood exactly what she was feeling—even if she wasn't completely sure herself. For right then, her heart burned with desire to know him better. She wanted to lean toward him, even rest her head on his broad shoulder.

But the yearning was all mixed up with a need to see Daniel again. He'd broken up with her, but she wanted to see him face-to-face. She wanted to read whatever was in his eyes. She now knew that his letter wasn't enough.

Ach, but she was confused.

"You got a letter from him?" Luke asked.

She nodded.

"I see," he said slowly. "But you want to see him."

He didn't ask her; he simply stated it as fact. Once more, she wondered how he knew what she was feeling.

Again, she nodded.

"You should go home."

She shook her head. "My *dat* won't allow it. Not yet."

"Then Daniel should come here."

She gaped at him. "*Aenti* would never agree. Never."

Luke was silent for a long moment.

Her mind whirled. Luke had stated what she knew in her heart she needed. She needed to see Daniel. But could it be possible? Could Daniel come to Linder Creek long enough for them to have a conversation?

"But ... how?" she murmured.

Luke shrugged. "I don't know. Maybe he has some business in town, and you could meet with him for a bit."

"But... My *dat* wouldn't approve."

He said nothing. He was an Amish man, and he should have immediately sided with her father and his authority over her, but he didn't. He merely shrugged again. She studied him. Never had she known an Amish man like him. She knew he was devout; she knew he was loyal... But somehow, he seemed to allow for a woman to think for herself—to make some decisions for herself.

It was an unsettling idea to her, but she appreciated it. She liked it. Were there other Amish men like him? She knew different districts had different levels of strictness. Yet Linder Creek was quite conservative—like Hollybrook.

Luke was different from any man she'd ever come into contact with before. Her admiration for him rose the longer she thought on it.

This time, it was she who reached out and touched his sleeve. He looked down quickly as if she'd burned him with her touch. Then he glanced up at her, and for a moment, she let herself be lost in his eyes. And then, she trembled and blinked.

"I will see him," she said. "I will write to him and ask him to have some business in town."

Luke nodded slowly and a fleeting look of dread filled his eyes, but then it was gone, and he was smiling at her again.

"*Gut.*" He snapped the reins and clicked his tongue at his horse. The buggy sped up. "I'm glad you'll get to see him."

THE BROKEN ENGAGEMENT

Anna knew he liked her. He wanted to court her—he'd said so. So why in the world was Luke glad she was going to see Daniel? It didn't make any sense at all. But she felt better. Immensely better, knowing she would get to see Daniel soon. She would get to hear things from his actual lips... She would get to look into his actual eyes...

Luke turned quiet, which was so out of character—but not for long. Within ten minutes, he had her laughing again as they chatted and compared stories about their hometowns. Their afternoon trip became totally entertaining as Luke half-invented stories about everything they passed.

Anna was able to fully relax and enjoy herself, which felt awfully good. When Luke took her back to Claire's, she didn't want to get out of the buggy. Yet, she needed to write to Daniel—needed to ask him to please come up with some reason to visit Linder Creek, so she bade Luke farewell after he'd carried Claire's repaired bridle into the barn.

Daniel stared at Anna's letter. He was stunned she'd written again after his last letter of rejection, and he was even more stunned by what she was asking him to do. He tried to imagine her writing this letter, tried to imagine her biting her lip in concentration, tried to imagine her brow furrowing with intent.

She wanted to see him. At first glance, he'd been excited, but that excitement was quickly replaced by dread. He didn't want to see her, not really. He especially didn't want to see her in the library. Had she forgotten that the Linder Creek Public Library was where he had written the articles? He hardly wanted to go back there. And truthfully, he didn't want to drag out their end by seeing her at all—no matter where they were meeting. They were over, and he was at peace with it. Why have to say it all over again? He feared hurting Anna even further than he already had.

Yet, he couldn't ignore her request. So, he sat down on his bed and worked to come up with a plan.

Chapter Fifteen

Anna didn't want to deceive Claire, but she couldn't see any way around it. Daniel was going to be in Linder Creek that afternoon, and he'd be waiting for her at the public library. Anna could hardly explain that to Claire, so she'd been forced to ask for Luke's help. After all, this whole meeting had been his idea in the first place.

"Where did you say you were going?" Claire asked Anna, smoothing down her apron as she rested on the davenport. "And will you be back for supper?"

"*Jah*, I should be back well before supper. Don't fret, *Aenti*, I'll have it ready at the regular time."

"I ain't fretting, child. Simply asking a question."

"Luke is taking me into town. I think he wants to buy me something at the bakery."

"So, you are courting now?" Claire couldn't keep the pleasure from her face.

Anna sighed. "Not officially."

"Officially or not, you've been seeing an awful lot of the man. It pleases me, Anna. For sure and for certain. I reckon your *dat* will be right pleased, too."

"Have you told him?" Anna asked, alarmed.

"*Nee*, not yet."

"I-I can tell him later," Anna said. "Please don't you tell him."

Claire's eyes narrowed, and she studied Anna for a moment before answering. "Fine. But I see no reason not to set his mind at ease."

Ach, but her father's mind wouldn't be at ease if he knew where she was really going that afternoon. Stifling a wave of guilt, Anna went to get her coat and scarf. "I'll see you soon, *Aenti,*" she said and slipped outside.

Luke hadn't even arrived yet, but Anna couldn't stay in the house another minute. She walked down the drive, deciding to wait for Luke there. It was odd asking him to help her with this. She was aware of the irony, considering Luke's intentions toward her. But she couldn't come up with any other idea that Claire wouldn't question.

And Luke had been a good sport about it. Surprisingly good, Anna thought.

She stood beside the mailbox, peering down the road. Within moments, she saw his buggy turn onto the asphalt from the next drive. When she could make out his face, she saw that he was smiling—albeit not quite as widely as normal.

He pulled the buggy to a stop, and she hurried around to jump in.

"I told *Aenti* that you were going to buy me something at the bakery," she said nervously, without even greeting him first.

He nodded. "Then I'll buy you something."

"I—" She stopped short. "*Ach,* I wasn't suggesting that you should—"

He held up a hand. "I know you're uneasy about this, and I know you don't like to tell untruths. So, I will buy you something." He smiled then, an easier, warmer smile. "Besides, I would like to buy you a goodie."

She let out the breath she hadn't known she was holding. "All right. Thank you, Luke." Tears filled her eyes. "And thank you for this. All of this."

He didn't look at her. "I'm happy to help," he said.

They made the rest of the trip to town in silence. He drove straight to the library.

"I'll wait for you in the parking lot, and then we'll go to the bakery."

She swallowed past the lump in her throat. "All... all right." He reached across her to open her door and she couldn't help but breathe him in. His now familiar scent calmed her nerves and served to bolster her seriously flagging courage.

She climbed out of the buggy. "I don't know how long—"

"Doesn't matter," he interrupted. "I'll be here."

She swallowed again and nodded. And then she turned to go into the library.

Although Luke had pointed out the library on her tour the other day, they hadn't gone inside. Anna stood for a moment, getting her bearings. Then she turned toward what appeared to be a somewhat private reading area, complete with a throw rug, easy chairs and a few tables. Once she headed toward it, she saw Daniel standing behind one of the chairs. He appeared to see her at the exact moment she saw him.

Her breath caught and her legs began to shake. He lifted his hand in a wave and moved toward her. They met in front of one of the tables, and Anna searched his face. It was so familiar, that for a moment, she was transported back in time, to the days when they were still together, before any of this had happened. A fondness for him enveloped her and she smiled now, her stomach relaxed.

"Anna," he said.

She inhaled and tensed up again. Her name on his lips didn't sound the same anymore. The previous intimacy or was it joy, wasn't there anymore. It was … it was just her name.

"D-Daniel." She glanced around and they sat beside one another on a small sofa. "Thank you for coming."

"I needed to," he said slowly. "I think you were right in asking me. It didn't seem proper to break up with you by letter."

She was watching him closely. Studying every expression. Trying to read what was in his eyes. And it was odd—she couldn't do it. Normally, she would have known what he was thinking before he spoke. Sometimes, she would finish his sentences for him. But now, looking into his eyes, there was a barrier there. He wasn't going to reveal everything to her. Not anymore.

At first, she was disturbed by it, and she wanted to push her way in, but something stopped her. She leaned back against the cushion of the sofa. The burning desire to know his thoughts diminished. She took a long slow breath. She felt only fondness for him. The kind of fondness one felt for someone who'd once been close but wasn't anymore.

His gaze hadn't left hers, and she saw a knowing spread over his face.

"It was right," he said softly. "Us breaking up. You see it now. Feel it."

Her eyes welled with tears and she nodded.

"I'm sorry, Anna. Truly."

"I know you are." She took another slow breath. "How are you, Daniel? I mean, really?"

"I've been better," he said, mustering a smile. "But it's going to be all right. I've learned a lot."

"I don't see how Freddie—"

He shook his head, cutting her off. "I know. I don't see how, either. But it's going to be all right. Somehow, I know it is. And I know myself a whole lot better now, too." He shrugged. "A hurtful way to accomplish it, but there it is. I won't... I won't be so foolish again."

"I would have stood by you," Anna said. "I didn't want to leave Hollybrook."

"I know you would have. And I know you didn't want to leave. But I'm glad now. Oh, I wasn't at first. But your *dat* was right to send you away. If you... If you want to come back home now, I won't contact you. Your *dat* wouldn't have to worry."

A tear fell down her cheek. She shuddered, knowing she would never feel the same way about him again, and mourning that. But this Daniel... He was still a fine man, as she had always believed him to be, yet there was a new depth to him. He had changed. And she knew—just as he did—that it was going to be all right for him. A heaviness left her spirit, and relief spread through her, filling her and bringing her peace.

"I was worried about you..." she said. "I feel better now. Now that I see you with my own eyes."

He gave a soft laugh.

She went on. "You traveled a long way to see me today. Thank you."

"It wasn't so long. I would do it again." He touched her hand. "Thank you for everything. We were... Well, we had something special, didn't we?"

Another tear slipped down her cheek. "We did, Daniel. We did."

She stared into his dear eyes and wished she could give him a hug good-bye. She didn't dare—for they were in public, and besides, it wasn't their way. But she wanted to. She wanted to feel his arms around her one last time. She reached out and clasped his hand.

"Thank you, Daniel. I pray your future will be blessed."

"As I pray for yours," he said softly, clasping her hand in turn. Then he let go and stood. "*Gut*-bye, dear Anna."

"So soon?" she asked, standing now, too.

"There is nothing more to say."

"Daniel?"

"*Jah?*"

"When I do come back to Hollybrook, I will greet you when I see you. Gladly. Despite the silencing."

THE BROKEN ENGAGEMENT

His eyes misted over, and he nodded. Then without another word, he turned, and left her staring after him.

∼

It took a moment before Anna moved. It was as if she needed to let her last meeting with him settle into her mind—process it somehow. It was over; truly and completely over. But it wasn't as if it hadn't happened. It had happened. And the memories of it would be cherished. In that way, Daniel would always be part of her life, part of her experience.

But as she stood there in the library, as she heard muffled conversations here and there, as she saw the flicker of the electric light overhead, as she felt the even heat of an *Englisch* building, she knew the finality of one relationship and the hopeful beginnings of another.

It was *all right*—it was all right for her to feel something for Luke Miller. And she did feel something. She liked him. More than liked him, in truth. And there didn't have to be one bit of guilt in that. Not anymore. She smiled softly and began walking toward the door of the library. When she pushed through, she saw Luke had left the buggy and was leaning against the brick wall, waiting for her. He saw her and straightened immediately, smiling.

"Anna," he said.

She walked to him. "I'm ready to go to the bakery."

He studied her for a minute and then his smile deepened. "Are you now?"

She nodded. "I am."

Epilogue

These last six months have held so many things and brought so many changes, that sometimes, my head spins. Everything changed after Daniel was caught with his writing. Everything changed after I met Luke Miller. And then everything changed again after the last time I saw Daniel at the library in Linder Creek.

It always puzzled me how willing Luke was to help me arrange that meeting. It didn't really make sense because I knew Luke liked me. Why would he help me meet with another man—particularly one I'd been engaged to?

I didn't ask him right away. I was embarrassed to—I thought it would seem presumptuous of me. But later, I did ask him. He looked at me for a long time with those dark blue eyes of his. And then a smile tugged at his lips.

"What?" I asked. "What's so funny?"

"Not a thing," he told me. "I'm not smiling because something's funny. I'm smiling because... Well, first of all, you look so completely adorable looking at me, and secondly, because me helping you did exactly what I prayed it would."

My eyes narrowed. "What do you mean?"

"Ahh, Anna. I love you. I do. I love you. I've loved you since I first met you, I think. But I had to be sure you were free. And you were suffering then, not being able to see Daniel. Not being able to talk about your relationship face-to-face. I figured you needed to see him. You had to. And it could have gone one of two ways. You'd see him and realize how much you still loved him and wanted to be with him. Or ... and this was what I prayed for ... you'd see him and realize that it was over."

I stared at him. "That was a big risk."

"I know. I about died waiting for you outside the library that day. Truth be told, I could hardly breathe. And then I saw Daniel—well, I assumed it was Daniel—leave the building. I studied him, trying to read his face, and he didn't look like a man who was still engaged. Then I started to breathe again. You took a while to come out. That made me nervous, but as soon as you came through the door, I could see it was me. It was me you wanted to be with."

I slapped his shoulder, then, playfully. "You did not see that."

"*Jah*, I did," he claimed.

I started to laugh. "All right. Maybe you did. Goodness, but you've got a big head."

He really laughed then. "That I do, my dearest Anna. But only where you're concerned."

And that is how we are. We have fun together, teasing each other, enjoying the day. But there are serious moments, too. Yet even so, somehow, they're better with Luke.

Everything is better with Luke.

We're engaged now. We're not published yet, of course, not until late fall, close to our wedding date in November. *Dat* and *Mamm* are right happy about it. My sisters, too, as they'll be my *newehockers* at the wedding. There was some confusion with my sisters at first, as they still thought of me being with Daniel. But *Dat* put an end to their confusion right quick-like. I'm not even sure what he said, but it never came up again.

I have to confess that when I returned to Hollybrook, I still felt resentment toward *Dat*. I knew in my head it was because of him that I met Luke, and I'm eternally grateful for that. But I had trouble getting over the way *Dat* banished me from my own home. As the weeks have passed, though, I've been able to slowly put it down. It's *Dat's* way—as it is the way of so many men in our district. It's such a contrast to Luke. I love the way he listens to my opinions and considers them important—and my thoughts can actually have an influence over him and us.

Truly, I like that so much better.

Luke and I write a lot of letters these weeks. Being apart is hard. But once harvest is over, he's going to move temporarily to Hollybrook, staying with our neighbors and helping out as he can on their farm. He'll be here until after the wedding. Then, we'll move to Linder Creek and live with his *mamm*. That suits me fine, as I like her very much. Even being next door to Claire will be nice. After all the time I spent with her, I grew to appreciate her better. She's still thorny around the edges, but she does approve of me now, and that helps.

THE BROKEN ENGAGEMENT

Of course, she is over the moon about Luke and me, taking personal credit for us being together. Ha!

I haven't seen much of Daniel. I did run into him in town one day early on, and I greeted him warmly. He was more subdued, but I felt his good wishes.

The best news, though, is that his silencing is over. Two weeks ago, an *Englisch* woman came to town looking for Freddie. I know this because, *ach*, how the tongues have wagged. Anyway, we all finally know what happened, and that it was Freddie who lied. This woman tried to see Freddie, but he denied knowing her. She tried to get past his folks to speak to him, but it did no *gut*. That made her so angry that she stormed into town and began talking to anybody who would listen.

Unfortunately, one of those people who would listen was Sarah Kriper, who has a mouth and a willingness to use it bigger than Edmund's Pond.

As it was told, Freddie and this woman had been in a relationship. She fell into the family way, and Freddie became desperate and wanted money to... to...

I can't write it. I just can't. It breaks my heart.

But the woman is no longer in the family way. She even claimed Freddie paid her living expenses for a while. Freddie didn't dare tell Daniel the truth of it, or Daniel would never have agreed to get the money. After all this came out, I believe Freddie would have been shunned, except he has never joined church. But he's as *gut* as shunned now, anyway. *Ach*, but the people are upset with him. My heart hurts for the whole big mess.

But Daniel has been welcomed back with open arms and contrite hearts. Everyone knows he didn't lie, nor did he know what Freddie wanted and used the money for. I'm happy for Daniel. And for his folks. So now, the future looks brighter for Daniel, and I'm awful glad.

My future, too, is bright and full of promise. I am eager to be married, eager to make my home in Linder Creek, and eager to bear Luke's *bopplis*. I'll miss my family, for sure and for certain, but Linder Creek isn't so far away.

I have a lovely, growing stack of letters from Luke. In truth, I must admit I re-read them all the time. So much so that some are becoming quite tattered. His words always make me smile, and often, I'll laugh right out loud. One time, my sister Prudence came in and asked me what in the world I was laughing at.

"My Luke," I told her. "He has a way of saying things…"

"Can I read it?" she asked, pointing to the letter I was holding.

I smiled at her. "I think I'll keep it private. But don't worry, one day you'll have your own beau who makes you smile and laugh."

"Do you think so?" she asked wistfully.

"I do."

Satisfied, she slipped from my room. I watched her go, knowing that if she's blessed even half as much as I am, she'll be a fortunate girl, indeed.

The End

Continue Reading...

Thank you for reading **The Broken Engagement!** Are you wondering **what to read next?** Why not read **Minding His Nephews. Here's a peek for you:**

Nancy Jantzi squeezed the dishrag and draped it over the edge of the sink. She turned to Alma, one of her four young sisters who was repeatedly tapping a wooden spoon on an empty pan.

"Please stop that," she said, trying to keep the impatience from her voice. "I can't even hear myself think."

Alma stopped and stared at her. "But it sounds like real music, don't it? Like them *Englisch* folks on their phones."

Nancy sighed. "It sounds like you beating a spoon on a pan."

Alma's face crumpled, and Nancy immediately regretted her harsh words. "I'm sorry, Alma. You're right. It does sound like music."

"I don't see why we can't have guitars and such," Alma, who at only seven years old, was already decrying what she felt was unjust. "I think *Gott* likes guitars."

Nancy suppressed a grin. She was often either amused or chagrinned by how Alma phrased things "Oh, you do, do you?"

"*Jah*. They're right pretty. I want one."

Nancy's brow rose. "You know you're not getting a guitar, Alma. You may as well put that to rest right now."

"I asked for one for Christmas."

"And you didn't get it, did you?" Nancy softened her tone. "You know we don't go much for Christmas gifts, anyway."

"I don't see why not," Alma said, setting her jaw. "Other folks get presents."

"*Ach,* you're in a mood. Why not go see what our sisters are up to?"

"I don't want to be watching over them. I'm always watching them."

Nancy stepped forward and gave her sister a playful jab. "Now, did I say to go watch over them? *Nee,* I didn't. I bet they're up to something right fun, and here you are, complaining and missing out."

Alma cracked a smile then. "I s'pose."

"They're likely playing hide and seek upstairs..." Nancy suggested.

With that, Alma flew out of the kitchen, and Nancy heard her scramble up the steps. She smiled. Her four sisters were considerably younger than her nineteen years. Nancy's mother, Janine, had suffered numerous miscarriages between Nancy and the younger ones. Nancy had been old enough to be aware of most of them—something that had broken her heart right along with her mother's and father's.

VISIT HERE To Read More!
https://ticahousepublishing.com/amish.html

Thank you for Reading

If you **love Amish Romance**, **Visit Here:**

https://amish.subscribemenow.com/

to find out about all **New Hollybrook Amish Romance Releases! We will let you know as soon as they become available!**

If you enjoyed **The Broken Engagement,** would you kindly take a couple minutes to leave a positive review on Amazon? It only takes a moment, and positive reviews truly make a difference. I would be so grateful! Thank you!

Turn the page to discover more Amish Romances just for you!

More Amish Romance for You

We love clean, sweet, rich Amish Romances and have a lovely library of Brenda Maxfield titles just for you! (Remember that ALL of Brenda's Amish titles can be downloaded FREE with Kindle Unlimited!)

If you love bargains, you may want to start right here!

VISIT HERE to discover our complete list of box sets!

https://ticahousepublishing.com/bargains-amish-box-sets.html

VISIT HERE to find Brenda's single titles.

https://ticahousepublishing.com/amish.html

About the Author

I was blessed to live part-time in Indiana, a state I shared with many Amish communities. I now live in Costa Rica. One of my favorite activities is exploring other cultures. My husband, Paul, and I have two grown children and five precious grandchildren. I love to hole up in our mountain cabin and write. You'll also often find me walking the shores by the sea. Happy Reading!

https://ticahousepublishing.com/

Made in the USA
Coppell, TX
27 March 2021